Notions of Murder
Mibs Monahan Mysteries #2

By Joan L. Kelly

Full Quiver Publishing
Pakenham, ON

Notions of Murder (Mibs Monahan Mysteries #2)
Copyright 2022 Joan L. Kelly

Published by
Full Quiver Publishing
PO Box 244
Pakenham, Ontario K0A 2X0
www.fullquiverpublishing.com

ISBN Number: 978-1-987970-39-5
Printed and bound in the USA
Cover design: James Hrkach
Cover model: Evelina Zhu

NATIONAL LIBRARY OF CANADA
CATALOGUING IN PUBLICATION

Published by FQ Publishing
A Division of Innate Productions

This book is dedicated to men and women who bravely step forward to protect and serve. Thanks, appreciation, and admiration go to those who serve in the various branches of the military and all police and law officers, firefighters, and emergency personnel.

It is also dedicated to the faithful civilians who give with their time, talents, and determination. Fathers, mothers, grandparents, brothers, sisters, married and single, women and men. Anyone who faces the day-to-day challenges of life, taking up their daily burdens to make this world a better place.

I would like to give a special dedication to members of my family, past and present, who have served their country with honor. There have been many over the past two hundred and fifty years, from Israel Meadows and Mathias Horn, who served in the Western Frontier during the American Revolution, and Martin Henry Smith, who fought with the 117th Illinois Infantry during the American Civil War, to the three dozen or more family members who served in various branches of the military: WWI, WWII, Korea, Vietnam, Iraq, Afghanistan, as well as stateside and the Peace Corps. Also, those who worked in law enforcement, firefighting, medical emergency positions, or chose a life as a priest.

It is a family heritage to be proud of.

Chapter 1

The mahogany-colored Belgian Malinois stepped softly around the bales of straw, slipping ghostlike along the rough wooden wall. With a signal from her partner, Shadow stopped and immediately lowered her body to the floor. Scooting slowly forward until she was next to Willy's side, the military-trained, multipurpose canine waited for further instructions. Chocolate-colored eyes were surrounded by a black-masked face and watched patiently as William McBride snapped pictures on his phone.

When he finished, Willy stepped back carefully and motioned to Shadow. The duo made their way past the bales and crept down a steep, narrow set of stairs. They had almost reached the door when they heard a slight noise to the right. Willy turned and saw a chunky man in worn jeans and a stained work shirt come around the far end of a shelving unit.

"Hey! Son of a...!" the man exclaimed. Turning back, he yelled to someone behind him.

Willy yanked the door open and quickly headed down the alley.

Despite a slight limp, Shadow took the lead and reached the delivery truck parked around the corner shortly before her owner.

Clicking the key fob to unlock the vehicle's

cab, Willy pulled open the door and signaled to the dog. He watched as Shadow made a smooth jump, got in, and moved to the passenger seat. Willy climbed up, started the engine, and sped into the adjacent road. The driver blew out a long breath as they made their escape.

"Do you think we lost them?" Willy often talked to his loyal dog, his partner. "We'd better take the information we have to the authorities. Now that they saw us, those criminals may move their activities. We can't wait and let that happen." Willy smiled when he glanced at Shadow, who kept her eyes on him, watching as if she knew something important was happening. "I'm glad we made all our deliveries early so we can drop off the truck and get over to the police station."

Fifteen minutes later, Willy pulled the delivery truck into its assigned parking spot behind the warehouse belonging to Sims' Wholesale Sewing Distributors. Pulling out his phone and checking the names on his contact list, Willy tapped the number for Jace Trueblood, a detective on a nearby police force. He attached the pictures and hit send. Willy climbed out of the cab with the intent of hurrying into the office and dropping off the keys and inventory papers. He let Shadow jump to the ground, then shut the door. Willy moved around the back of the vehicle and waited as the images were in the process of sending. Shadow growled, so Willy stopped and studied his partner. She only growled like that when she sensed danger.

The next moment, Willy felt himself falling as two excruciatingly painful blows hit him in the back. As the light around him began to fade, he saw his phone lying a few inches from his fingers, his mind easing when he saw the word *sending* change to *sent*. William McBride, former Navy officer, part of a special forces combat-craft crew, had survived numerous life-threatening missions overseas. Now, he mumbled his last words, "Jesus, my Savior, I am heartily sorry for having offended Thee…Who art all good…"

~~

The dog gave a deep whine as she lay on the ground by the fallen man's side. The whine changed to a vicious growl as the killer approached and pointed the gun at the man's head. The animal made a long jump and sunk its teeth deep into the attacker's arm.

"Ah! Get it off me!" the man yelled. The dog tore flesh and drew blood as the killer tried to shake her loose. "Do something," the man pleaded with his partner. "Shoot the dog! Get it off me."

The second shooter aimed as the dog struggled and jerked. "Shut up," he instructed the first man. "What's the point of using a silencer if you're going to yell?" Stepping closer, the second shooter pulled the trigger. A popping sound came from the gun, and the dog fell to the ground.

Hissing at the first man, he said, "You're bleeding all over. You'll leave DNA evidence."

The first man pulled off his worn sweatshirt, wiped the spots of blood that had dripped onto the ground, and then wrapped the shirt around his bleeding arm.

The second man touched the fallen driver's neck, searching for a pulse. "The guy's dead. Let's get out of here." He smashed his heel onto the dead man's phone. He started to walk away but stopped and reached down, grabbing the broken phone.

~~

"Please, step back!" a uniformed officer directed the small crowd gathered in the parking lot.

As he drove closer, Sergeant McCormick's trained eyes took in the scene: several people seemed visibly shaken as other officers interviewed them. Others appeared to have been drawn to the area out of curiosity, milling around, gawking. An EMS van and two police cars were positioned around the crime scene, and a policewoman quickly stretched a yellow crime scene tape across a section of the lot. With McCormick was his associate, Detective Jacoby. They'd pulled up and parked beside the emergency vehicles.

Accepting the crime scene booties and gloves handed to him, Sergeant McCormick slipped them on. Unbuttoning his suit jacket and watching where he placed his feet, the sergeant squatted down by the victim and shook his head. "Shot in the back. This guy didn't have a chance to react or get out of the way." After viewing the body, he got up and carefully scanned the surrounding area. Turning toward his associate, he pointed to a nearby dumpster. "Jacoby, is that blood?"

Both men carefully stepped closer to what appeared to be a blood trail leading to a dumpster.

McCormick motioned to one of the policemen. Noting his name tag, he asked, "Did anyone check the trash dumpster, Officer Bitter?"

"Yes, sir," Bitter answered. "I saw the spots of blood and checked inside. The container is only slightly full, and there doesn't appear to be any blood in there. We'll have the forensic team do a thorough exam when they get here."

McCormick continued to study the blood for a moment longer. "How about under or behind?" He questioned.

Bitter shrugged. "There isn't enough room for a person to fit, but let's see what we have."

Bitter and Jacoby pushed the dumpster forward.

A weak growl came from the shadows. "Whoa, easy, buddy," Detective Jacoby whispered in a soothing voice. Without turning away, he said, "There's a dog back here. I think he's in bad shape."

As they moved the trash bin further, the dog

lifted its head and whimpered softly.

"Have one of the emergency technicians come over here," Jacoby instructed Officer Bitter.

McCormick tapped Detective Jacoby on the arm. "Notice his mouth? I believe there is a piece of material caught in his teeth."

"You need me?" a voice asked.

The two detectives recognized the woman holding a medical kit as she walked toward them. Studying the technician wearing a t-shirt with the EMS emblem on it, McCormick said, "Yes, Ann. See if you can help our witness."

She pointed to the injured animal. "The dog is a witness?"

Jacoby moved out of the way to allow her to get closer.

Sergeant McCormick brushed a tiny piece of dust off his suit before answering. "I believe he may be the only witness we have." Pointing to the canine's mouth, he requested, "If you can do it without getting bitten, we need that piece of cloth. Also, do a swab around the teeth."

The woman, whose ID lanyard named her as Ann Johnson, spoke softly to the dog and slowly held out her gloved hand, moving it along the animal's ribcage. "Let's see where all this blood is coming from." She worked carefully to try to stop the bleeding before standing up and eyeing the detectives.

"Is he going to make it?" McCormick asked.

"It's a she," Johnson corrected, "and according to the dog tag, her name is Shadow. I stopped the bleeding, but I suggest that you get her to a veterinarian ASAP. She has a bullet hole just below the ribcage." She shook her head. "I don't know what happened to this dog in the past, but she has scars all over her body."

As he watched Ann write something down, Sergeant McCormick tilted his head, and he pondered the technician's words. The detective automatically adjusted his tie and rebuttoned his jacket. McCormick was a fastidious dresser, but he was better known for his observation and deductive powers.

Ann handed two evidence bags to the detective. "There is also a phone number on her tag. I wrote it down for you." The EMT held out a slip of paper.

McCormick motioned Officer Bitter to his side. "Find out where the nearest animal hospital is and get this dog over there."

An employee of the medical examiner's office had arrived and was examining the deceased man.

"Anything other than the obvious, Dr. Barton?" Detective McCormick approached the septuagenarian, a veteran doctor who could have retired over five years ago.

Dr. Barton responded, "I won't make an official statement until I do a complete autopsy, but it appears that this man died from two gunshots to the back. Either one would have been fatal. I doubt if he lasted more than a few minutes." He stood up and crossed his arms. The M.E. carefully cut the deceased's shirt. "This isn't the first time this man has faced death." He pointed to several scars, including a long, narrow one on the upper part of the man's back. "I would say that scar is quite a few years old and was the result of a knife wound; just missed the spinal cord."

Detectives McCormick and Jacoby glanced at each other as McCormick shook his head and wondered out loud. "Who have we got here?"

"Here's his wallet." One of the first on-the-scene officers passed an evidence bag to the detective. "He was a delivery driver for the warehouse here." The officer indicated the building they stood behind. "I told the owner and foreman that we would need to talk to them. We've been interviewing some of the other employees, but they haven't given us any useful information other than the man's name." Jerking his head toward the building, he said, "There are no security cameras back here, unfortunately."

McCormick used his gloved hand to take the wallet out of the bag. He read from a driver's license, *McBride, William Andrew.* Jacoby pointed to a small card sticking out of the billfold.

"Look at the police emblem on that business card," the detective said.

McCormick shifted his eyes from the license and slid out the business card. One eyebrow arched in question as he considered the information in front of him. "Why does our victim have the name and phone number of the Havendale Chief of Detectives?"

Chapter 2

Jace slid out of his truck and stretched. He liked Saturdays. Unless there was a case pending, like the car theft ring the Havendale Police team had recently thwarted, the detective typically had the day off. For the past couple of months, he had spent many of those Saturdays working on his old Georgian Colonial house inherited from his great-uncle, Ezekiel Trueblood. It had been so hot and humid recently that he couldn't work for too long at a time since his place didn't have air conditioning.

Even better, Monahan's Sewing Shop closed at one o'clock on Saturdays. His girlfriend, Mibs, would often come over after the shop closed and help him with the remodeling project for the day. Today he had worked in the yard for a few hours before cleaning up and heading over to Monahan's. A new movie had just come out. It was one that Mibs wanted to see, so they had agreed to have a late lunch and then go to the matinée at the local theater.

Jace had reached the building entrance before he remembered that he hadn't locked the doors of his truck. Chuckling to himself, he realized that he'd started falling into the habits of a small-town citizen. Not that long ago, when he still lived in a big city, locking his vehicle would have been automatic. Living in Havendale allowed him to enjoy a calmer, less stressful life. The tension he had previously felt, as well as his blood pressure, had gone down.

Moving away from Nashville had been a good decision. Less traffic, less stress, and a slower pace were all good things, but the best thing that had come from his relocation had been meeting Mibs. The demands of law enforcement: the long hours, the physical and mental angst of dealing with criminals, and a lot of paperwork, had made single life preferable to Jace. He had dated often enough but without letting himself become too close to any woman. He had not considered marriage as a likely part of his future. Now, he'd begun to rethink that idea.

He could not count the number of times during the day when her green eyes and soft smile would pop into his mind. He had a reputation as a tough and determined detective when solving crimes. He had developed the ability to put on a stoic, unreadable face when interviewing criminals, then change to a sympathetic demeanor when trying to elicit information from a witness or victim. Until he met Mibs, a smile hadn't affected him that much. She'd changed that. The pretty strawberry-blonde could turn to him with a tender expression in her eyes and he would melt inside. He was still trying to wrap his mind around the fact that anyone had found a way into his heart.

He remembered years ago when he and his brother, Connor, had entered their teenage years and wondered if they would catch the eye of any girls in their high school. The two brothers had been sitting at the kitchen table, teasing each other about their dateless status. Their grandma had strolled into the room and had commented, "There's a lid for every pot."

Conner had scrunched up his face and asked, "What does that mean?"

"Never mind," she had replied. "I'll start praying for your future spouse now. You'll know her when you meet her."

Connor had rolled his eyes. Jace had smiled.

For whatever reason, his grandmother's words came to mind now. He wondered if Grandma had actually recited those prayers. *Yeah, she probably did.* She had been gone for several years now, but he could still picture her sitting in her rocker, ruby-colored rosary beads threaded through her fingers. He sighed. It had been a long time since he'd thought of her.

His stomach clenched as images from his brother's funeral came to mind. Everyone praying. Too little. Too late. Reaching for the handle, Jace pulled open the door to Monahan's Sewing Shop and stepped through. As soon as he entered, he stopped and stared.

A young woman in an exquisitely beautiful wedding gown stood in the middle of the room. Pure, white material covered the girl's slender figure. A profusion of miniature white roses cascaded down the front of the dress, curving around the bottom in a delicate design. A sparkling crystal crown held sheer lace material on the girl's head, flowing to the floor in supple folds.

Mirabelle Monahan, better known as Mibs, seamstress and co-owner of the store, standing next to the bride-to-be, turned, and smiled. "Jace! Is it almost one o'clock already?" When he didn't answer immediately, she continued, "You better close your mouth and come in the rest of the way."

Clearing his throat and taking a breath, Jace shut the door. "I'm sorry. I didn't mean to intrude." He paused. "I can wait in the truck."

"You don't need to do that," Mibs reassured him. "Why don't you go up to the apartment and get a drink? There's some tea in the refrigerator. I'm almost done here."

Jace was so taken by the bride-to-be that it took a moment before he noticed the other women in the shop. If appearances were any indication, the older, matronly type was the mother of the bride. A young girl with shining eyes was likely a friend or relative. Jace nodded and greeted them with a hint of his southern accent coming through. "Good aft' noon, ladies."

He then waved to the older lady sitting in a chair and clutching a cane. "Hi, Bernice."

"Good afternoon, Jace." She grinned so

widely that it reached her eyes and emphasized the multitude of wrinkles she had earned over the past eighty-plus years.

He noted several dresses hung on a rack nearby, individually encased in clear, protective clothing bags. Each had a different design, but all of them were in coordinating hues of blue. He stepped carefully so his size 12 double-E boots did not tromp on the long, delicate train of the dress or even the protective sheet of material the girl stood on. Jace scooted past the group gathered for the dress fitting. He hesitated as he passed the girl in white. Nodding, he said, "You sure are pretty as a peach, miss."

A wide smile spread across the girl's glowing face. "Thank you!" A bright pink blush washed against her cheeks.

Jace slowed only long enough to wink at Mibs, who had a cloth measuring tape around her neck and a small, tomato-shaped cushion chock-full of pins on her wrist. He mouthed a greeting, "Hey, sweetheart," before heading to the back of the store. Suddenly exuberated, he took two steps at a time to the upstairs.

~~

Thirty minutes later, Mibs climbed the stairs to her small efficiency apartment. Stepping through the door, she scanned the room for her full-time detective, part-time carpenter boyfriend. She didn't see him, but she did hear a mixture of a snore and sigh coming from the living room area. She walked around to the front of the sofa and found Jace sleeping with the television turned low to a ballgame, his boots off and nestled on the floor near the end of the couch, and a half-empty glass of iced tea sitting on the coffee table. The tough-as-nails First Sergeant Chief of Detectives appeared amazingly peaceful in sleep. Mibs didn't have the heart to wake him.

Jace and the other Havendale Police Force members, the detectives, the police officers, and even the office personnel had been working overtime. A few months ago, a gang from a neighboring, larger town had decided to set up a *chop shop* in their small, usually peaceful community. When a confidential informant let Detective Trueblood know about the activity, he and his team decided to disrupt that plan. They were not going to let those thugs bring stolen cars to their town, disassemble them, and ship the parts to other places. The team had to work long hours over the last few weeks, and their efforts had paid off. The *shop* barely got off the ground before it was shut down and the criminals locked behind bars.

Only the thought that she might wake him stopped Mibs from brushing back the wayward curls that had fallen across his forehead.

Mibs also knew that he spent much of the free time that he did have on remodeling the large fixer-upper that he now called his home. She relished those times when she could join him in his carpentry work and help bring new life into the old house. She thought about the good times they'd shared since she'd returned from college and opened Monahan's Sewing Shop. Slowly, her smile faded as she remembered the not-so-good times, too.

Mirabelle Monahan had first met Jace Trueblood shortly after he'd moved to Havendale as he investigated the deaths of two elderly sisters. Mibs had a strong sense of justice and wouldn't take no for an answer, at least not when she'd known she was right. Mibs was certain that Jennifer Morris' death hadn't been an accident, nor did she think that Jasmine Hornsby committed suicide. Insisting that Detective Trueblood investigate put them at odds at first. It also put Mibs in danger. Eventually, the murders of the two sisters were solved—the killer paying the ultimate price.

The months since then had brought Mibs and Jace closer together. According to Aunt Bernie, "The two were meant for each other."

This would be a great chance to take a quick shower. Mibs tip-toed to the bathroom with a fresh set of clothes and quietly shut the door. A short time later, she exited the bathroom wearing jeans and a pale-yellow cotton shirt with a butterfly motif circling the collar and sleeves. Her hair now hanging loose around her shoulders, she felt fresh, revitalized, and happy.

~~

Jace sat on the sofa, waiting. He let his gaze

linger on the attractive woman standing in front of him. Her strict upbringing and moral standards would not put up with him getting "too cheeky," a term his mother occasionally used. But he couldn't help teasing Mibs sometimes just to see her blush. "Ya shoulda woke me up. I could have given you a hand getting ready."

The expected blush showed up, but so did hands on her hips and her signature squared shoulders. "Watch what you say, mister, or you aren't going anywhere except home." Mibs glared, which just made Jace smile more.

"Yes, ma'am. I'll behave," he promised, chuckling.

Mibs shook her head and, after taking a glass out of the overhead cabinet, she opened the refrigerator to retrieve the iced tea. "I'm sorry I worked later than expected. I guess we won't get to the two o'clock movie."

"Nope. Not if we want to stop to eat," Jace replied. "We can try for the four o'clock show. Or we could hurry over to the movie now and eat afterward."

As soon as he said that, Mibs' stomach gave a noticeable rumble. She blushed for the second time.

Jace's grin grew wider. "I guess we'd better stop and eat first. You're hungry."

Nodding, Mibs said, "I missed my midmorning snack and coffee. It's been non-stop since we opened this morning." She tipped her glass up and quickly finished the drink.

Jake's grin grew in amazement as he thought about the scene he had encountered earlier. "You actually made that beautiful wedding dress?"

"Well!" Mibs crossed her arms. "Of course, I did. And the mother-of-the-bride's dress. And two bridesmaids' dresses. Who else could've made them? Did you think they grew on trees?"

Holding his hands up in surrender, he answered, "I didn't mean it that way. I just never thought about where women get their wedding dresses." He stepped close to Mibs. "It was gorgeous. You are amazin'. How long did it take to make it...them?"

"I've been working on them for about twelve weeks. It took a lot of overtime to get them done that quickly, considering there were three dresses plus the wedding gown." Mibs took a deep breath, then let it out. "I'm so glad the bride's dress fit perfectly and she could take it with her today. As much as I loved making it, I'm ready to move on to something else." She picked up her purse. "And, I *am* starving!"

This time, Jace laughed out loud. Pulling Mibs close, he gazed into her sparkling emerald eyes, leaned down, and gave her a gentle kiss before moving away. "Well, then we'd better find something to eat, darlin'."

When they reached the front of the shop,

Bernice was sitting behind the counter. "I already checked the back door and turned off the lights in the office," she informed them. "Just go and have a good time."

"Are you sure that you don't want to come with us?" Jace offered, glancing past the white hair, wrinkles, and slightly stooped posture and into the bright hazel eyes.

"No, thank you." Bernice stood up and leaned on her cane. "I'm going to lock the door behind you, turn off the rest of the lights, and go to my room. I have plenty of food in the little refrigerator in the kitchenette," she assured them. "For now, I'm going to make some popcorn and have my own movie time."

"What are you planning on watching, Aunt Bernie?" Mibs asked. "John Wayne? Jimmy Stewart? Katherine Hepburn?"

Bernice shook her head. "Those are all good actors, but I'm in the mood for a movie with singing and dancing. I haven't watched *Brigadoon* or *Singin' in the Rain* for a long time. *Seven Brides for Seven Brothers* would be another good option."

A couple quick chirps from Jace's personal phone interrupted their conversation. He pulled the phone from his pocket and checked the number of the text. "Hmm, I don't recognize this number." He tapped the screen and scanned through the pictures. "What in Sam Hill is this?" he mumbled, eyes widened.

~~

"What's wrong, Jace?" Concern filled Mibs. Jace had shifted from the relaxed, fun-loving person who had shown up to take her on a date. His gaze fixed ahead, his demeanor changed. Detective Jace Trueblood had arrived.

Chapter 3

Pulling a different phone out of his back pocket, Jace regarded the two ladies in front of him. "Sorry, I have to check something out," he said. "Excuse me for a few minutes. I have to call the station." He stepped across the room and called the Havendale Police Department.

~~

"I wonder what that's about," Aunt Bernie pondered out loud.

Mibs sighed. "I don't know, but I have a feeling we aren't going to the movies today."

Mibs realized that if she planned to have Jace as a boyfriend, she needed to share him with the local police force. As the recently appointed Chief of Detectives for Havendale's Police Department, he was on call 24/7. Mibs wasn't thrilled with the idea, but she also understood that it played a part in who he was.

~~

Jace hit the speed-dial button on his police-issued phone and waited for the response. "Havendale Police Department."

"This is Jace Trueblood. I need to talk to Sergeant Long in the homicide division."

It took only a minute for the connection to go through. "This is Sergeant Brice Long. How can I help you?"

"Brice, this is Jace. I'm going to send you a

phone number. I need you to tell me who it belongs to. Make it quick, please. I'll stay on the line."

Sergeant Long used the reverse phone lookup app on his computer and retrieved the needed information. "Jace?"

"Yeah, whose number is it?" the detective asked.

"It belongs to William McBride," Brice replied. "Do you want the address?"

"Text it to me."

"What's going on?"

"I'm not sure yet. I'll get back to you when I find out." Jace hung up and used the other phone to give Willy a callback. As he waited, he mumbled, "What have you been up to, Willy? Does this have somethin' to do with that envelope you asked me to hold?" The phone didn't ring through.

Jace checked the address that Brice Long had sent him. Picturing the town of Broadly in his head, he knew that the address was a little over an hour away. Calling Sergeant Long back, Jace informed the desk sergeant that he'd emailed a set of pictures to the station. "Brice, get these printed out. I'll come by and pick them up shortly. I'm heading to the address you gave me. I think the guy who sent them may need assistance."

"Do you want me to ask a local unit in Broadly to meet you?"

"Let me go check it out first," Jace said.

Jace returned to where Mibs and Bernice

waited then cleared his throat. "Hey, Mibs...ah..."

"It's okay, Jace," Mibs interrupted. "You have to leave, don't you?"

He took her hand in his. "Sorry. This may be important. I need to find out."

"I know. It's your job." Mibs tried to smile. "We'll see the movie another time." Pulling him closer, she gave him a quick kiss before stepping back. "Just be careful!"

"Always," he promised. He waved at Bernice, then hurried out.

~~

Mibs followed him to the door and set the lock. She turned back and gave a crooked smile to her aunt. "Would you like some company while you watch your movie?"

"Of course, my dear," Aunt Bernie assured her. "I'll make extra popcorn."

"I believe I need a little more than popcorn," Mibs said as her stomach grumbled again. "I think I'll warm up some of that leftover casserole." She held out her arm so her aunt could grab it for added support. "Would you care to join me, Aunt Bernie?"

"I would be delighted," her aunt answered. "In fact, maybe I'll set out some cheese and crackers, too." Accompanying Mibs to the area beyond the counter, she asked, "Will you still want popcorn when we watch the movie?"

"Of course!" Mibs smiled at her aunt, knowing that popcorn was her favorite snack.

Mibs studied the woman who had raised her

from infancy. She noted the soft white hair, the age spots dotting her face and hands, the wrinkles that gave character to her still pretty face, and the hazel eyes. She also noticed the growing tiredness in the older woman's features and how she moved.

When they'd opened this sewing shop, Aunt Bernie was only supposed to help when she felt like it – do as much or as little as she wanted. But their business had picked up rapidly. The shop became increasingly busy selling materials, patterns, and notions—pins, needles, threads, buttons, and other sewing accessories. Orders for custom-made clothing increased, and alterations were coming in non-stop.

By the time they reached the mini kitchen area, Mibs had made a decision. "Aunt Bernie, I think we are going to hire some help."

~~

Bernice leaned in toward her niece, now walking beside her. "Hmm," she responded, trying to hide her overwhelming relief. "That might not be a bad idea." She had been trying to devise a way to make that same suggestion to Mibs. Her energy had depleted over the years, her bones ached, and her body tired easily. But Bernice Monahan had never been a quitter and was determined to keep going as long as her girl needed her, as long as she could get up each morning and put one foot in front of the other.

Yes, she thought, *help would be such a blessing.*

~~

Jace drove back to his house on Maple Street, just a few blocks away from Monahan's. Entering the front door, he hurried up the curved staircase to the recently remodeled master bedroom. He slid up the cover of an antique roll-top desk and pulled a sealed envelope from one of the cubby holes. Jace tapped it in his palm a few times, considering the wisdom of opening it. William McBride had given this envelope to him a few months ago, cryptically saying that if something happened, Jace should do what he thought best. He considered the pictures that had been downloaded to his phone. He also hadn't been able to reach William McBride. It was time to open the envelope that Willy had left in his charge. He grabbed a smooth, wooden letter opener and slid it along the flap of the envelope. The detective took out a piece of paper, along with three pictures. He began reading.

To whom it may concern,

If you are reading this, then I must not have been able to come back and take the information to the police myself. Please see that this gets to someone in law enforcement at the Broadly Police Department.

I believe I have inadvertently uncovered a drug operation. I want to act on what I saw. Before I do that, I want to have some proof and adequate information for the authorities to act on.

Enclosed, find photos showing the name of the company in question. I'll try to get more. Then I'll contact the police.

At the bottom of the page, William McBride had written the date, his name, and phone number. One of the pictures showed a panel truck with a logo on the side. The second had the profile of a man stepping out of the truck. The third was a picture of a license plate.

"Well, Willy," Jace said out loud, "I'd say the photos you sent me today are more than enough to start the wheels of justice rolling." He thought about the retired Navy veteran he had met only a few months ago but had come to like and admire. Jace hoped that the man was okay.

The detective pulled out his cell phone. His immediate superior, Lieutenant Hank Taylor, answered on the first ring even though he was off for the weekend.

"Jace, what's up?"

Jace explained the note and the photos and that he couldn't get hold of the truck driver, William McBride. "I want to go to Broadly and make sure Willy isn't in trouble. I'll take the note and photos with me, and stop and grab the other photos that Long is printing. When I get there, I'll find Willy, and we'll go to the police station together. If I can't find him, I'll turn the stuff over to their drug enforcement unit."

After pausing for a moment, the lieutenant said, "Okay, Jace. Call me tonight and let me know what you've found out."

Less than fifteen minutes later, Jace had changed into a suit and adjusted his tie. He connected his holster to his belt, slid in the police issue handgun, and then clipped on his badge. He stopped by the station, picked up the photos, and gave Sergeant Long a synopsis of where and why for the sudden trip. Approximately forty minutes after receiving the text from William McBride, Jace accelerated down the highway toward Broadly.

Chapter 4

Fifty minutes into the drive, Jace's phone rang through the hands-free app on his console. "Trueblood here."

"Hello, Detective Trueblood. This is Sergeant Michael McCormick from the Broadly Police Department," the voice stated.

Jace didn't have to use much imagination to realize that this call would be about Willy. "Hello, Sergeant. What can I do for you?"

There was a short hesitation on the other end. "Do you know a delivery driver named William McBride?"

"Yes," Jace responded. "I've been trying to get hold of him, but he isn't answering his phone. I'm driving to his address now."

"Are you friends?" the sergeant asked.

"Just acquaintances, but I trust the guy." Before the other detective could respond, Jace asked, "Has something happened to Willy?"

"What makes you ask that?" the Broadly detective questioned.

"Sergeant McCormick, I'm less than fifteen minutes from Broadly. I'll explain when I get there. Where do you want to meet?"

After another short pause, the Broadly detective answered, "William McBride is dead. I'm still at the crime scene. You can come here, or I'll head to his house after I'm done."

Jace sighed sadly. "Where are you now, and how long will you be there?"

A short time later, Jace pulled across the street from the warehouse where Sergeant McCormick had directed him. He strolled around to the back of the building and presented his badge to the officer stationed behind the police tape.

"Sergeant McCormick's expectin' me."

After checking his identification, the policewoman lifted the tape to let Jace duck under into the restricted area. A group was gathered around a delivery truck, so Jace made his way over and picked out the man he thought was the lead detective. Jace had spotted two men in suits, but something in the stance and the demeanor of the slightly shorter man stood out as being in charge. As Jace approached, both men turned and scrutinized him.

Jace wasn't surprised when the gray-suited man spoke first. "Chief of Detectives Trueblood?"

Jace pulled out his badge. "Yes. And are you Detective McCormick? Or do you prefer Sergeant?"

"Sergeant McCormick is fine," McCormick replied.

A gurney with the victim's body was rolled toward an ambulance with its back doors open. Jace pointed to the stretcher and asked, "May I see?"

McCormick hesitated for a moment before nodding.

Stopping the EMS technicians and

unzipping the body bag, Jace folded back the top edge and peered at the still face of William Andrew McBride. "Willy, why didn't you reach out to me sooner?" he whispered as he opened the black plastic bag further. Studying the damage to the murder victim's chest, Jace turned back to McCormick. "These are exit wounds. That means he was shot from behind." Jace zipped the body bag closed and stood back so that the emergency personnel could take the body away.

"You're correct – two bullets to the back. Probably didn't see it coming," McCormick said.

"Didn't see it coming," Jace repeated slowly and frowned. "That doesn't surprise me. If he'd had any warning of trouble, he would have reacted." Controlling the sadness that filled him, Jace said, "He wouldn't have gone down easy if given a chance."

"Okay, Trueblood. Let's talk." Gesturing to his car, he walked toward it, stopping long enough to instruct the other detective to take over at the scene.

As the ambulance pulled away, Jace followed McCormick to a late-model blue sedan.

Jace had almost reached the car when he stopped and glanced back. "Wait! Was there a dog with McBride?" he asked.

McCormick straightened, his eyes wide. "Yes, there was a dog. She's at a nearby veterinary hospital. From her dog tags, we surmised that she belonged to the deceased."

"Yeah, she did." His eyes focused on the departing ambulance. "I've never seen Willy without Shadow nearby. They're both retired military veterans, *partners*."

"That explains where she came from," McCormick said. "She's being treated for a bullet wound. We're hoping that the dog may have collected some evidence for us."

"How so?" Jace asked.

Pointing to the passenger door and indicating that Jace should get in, McCormick headed to the driver's side. "She had a piece of bloody material snagged in her teeth. Apparently, she got a chunk of the attacker before she went down."

The sergeant started the engine and carefully maneuvered out of the parking lot. "Okay if we stop for a cup of coffee?"

"Sounds good," Jace said. "I had planned to have a late lunch with my girl, but that didn't happen. Coffee would be a plus."

McCormick nodded. "Maybe you can get a sandwich to go with your coffee. I know a place."

A short time later, Jace sat with McCormick at a booth of a busy dinner. He took a long sip. "Mmm, good coffee." Setting his cup down, he pulled a small packet and an envelope out of his inside jacket pocket and slid them across the table. "These came from William McBride. They're self-explanatory. Give them a quick inspection, and then we can have that talk."

The waitress came back and set a plate down in front of Jace. While the other detective studied the pictures and letter, Jace alternately took bites of his sandwich and munched on salty chips.

"When did you get these?" Sergeant McCormick asked.

"The set of pictures in the packet were emailed to me at around one-forty today. The letter and three photos were in a sealed envelope that McBride had asked me to hold." Taking another bite of his sandwich, Jace chewed and swallowed.

He pointed toward the pictures. "After I received those today, and when I couldn't get hold of Willy, I opened the envelope he'd left with me."

McCormick tossed the letter down onto the table next to the pile of photos and picked up his cup of coffee. "The M.E. estimated that he died between one and two o'clock. He must have emailed these pictures shortly before he got shot. So, you figure they caught him taking pictures and came after him?"

"That would be my guess." Jace rubbed his chin. "Maybe he realized it. Maybe that's why he texted the pictures to me, or maybe it was a precautionary measure."

The waitress came by and topped off their coffee.

Jace asked for the bill and pulled out his wallet. "Willy has a daughter, a teacher somewhere. Has anyone contacted her?"

"Not yet, but the company where he worked, Sims Wholesales, gave us the name listed as next of kin. We'll have someone call on her."

Putting his elbows on the table and resting his chin on interlaced fingers, Jace contemplated for a moment. "Sergeant McCormick," he said. "I have vacation time built up. I'd like to help apprehend Willy's killers."

The Broadly detective sat back and frowned. "I don't think we need to bring in outside law enforcement."

"Didn't say you *needed* help." Jace pursed his lips. "I'm sayin' I want to be in on this. I feel an obligation." He sat back. "If you have any doubts about my abilities, you can check me out. I won't get in your way."

McCormick sat quietly for a full minute. "Okay. You can be my sidekick for a few days. But I *will* check you out."

"Wouldn't expect any less." Jace placed twenty dollars on the table and stood up.

Sergeant McCormick scooped up the pictures with the letter. "I'll keep these." He put them in his jacket. He tapped the packet in his coat. "These drug dealers who likely killed McBride will probably do one of two things." He raised one finger. "They shot him and took his phone. They may think they are still in the clear and keep their operation going." He held up a second finger. "Or they won't want to take any chances and will move their operation."

"Sounds reasonable," Jace agreed. "Which means we'll have to move quickly."

A short time later, Jace had retrieved his Chevy Silverado, called Lieutenant Taylor, and headed over to the Broadly Police Station. He parked his vehicle in the back section of the lot across from several police cars. Before heading inside, he pulled out his phone and called Mibs.

"Hello?" she answered on the first ring.

"Hi, Mibs."

"Jace, is everything all right?"

He sucked in a breath, then exhaled. "I thought you and Bernice would want to know." He paused. "Willy McBride is dead."

Hearing a soft moan, Jace frowned, wishing he were there to comfort her. "I'm so sorry. I know he was more than a delivery man to you two."

Willy had been making deliveries to Monahan's since the first week they opened. After unloading the shop's order, he would usually accept the coffee and sweet roll that Bernice and Mibs offered, sharing a few minutes of conversation with them. His dog, Shadow, loved the two ladies and the treats they fed her. He imagined that they would miss his visits.

Part of Jace wished that he had driven back to Havendale to give the sad information in person to the two "Monahan ladies," as Willy always called them. Mibs, as well as her aunt, had been through a lot in the last year. But he needed to be where he was. Since he kept a 'go' bag tucked away in his truck, going back to Havendale hadn't been necessary.

"What...happened?" Mibs asked.

"I guess Willy decided to take on one last mission," Jace explained. "It appears that he discovered a drug ring while making his deliveries. He began taking pictures, trying to get proof to turn over to the police. Someone must've seen him." Jace paused for a few seconds. "Willy was shot and killed."

"Oh, no," she whispered.

Jace could hear the sadness in her quiet voice. "Mibs, I'm gonna stay in Broadly for a while and work with their detectives. I want to help finish what Willy started and make sure his killer is apprehended and arrested. I'm not sure how long I'll be gone."

Mibs didn't respond for a few seconds. Finally, she said, "Okay. But, Jace, please, please be careful."

"Always! I'll try calling tonight, but don't worry if I can't. I'm not sure what kind of schedule I'll be on," Jace told her. "I'll call when I can. Bye, Mibs."

"Thank you for letting us know. Talk to you later, Jace."

~~

Mibs stared at the phone after he hung up until Bernice finally interrupted her thoughts.

"Mibs, what's wrong?" Aunt Bernie questioned.

Slowly setting her cell phone down, Mibs

shared the sad information. After sitting in silence for several minutes thinking about the passing of their friendly delivery man, the two ladies sighed simultaneously. Grieved, Mibs stood and stepped away from the chair she had been using in her aunt's bedroom as they finished watching a movie together. Deciding on a second movie didn't seem appropriate now.

Chapter 5

Rain splashed against the large window fronting Monahan's Sewing Shop. Mibs' mind drifted to thoughts of Jace. She had heard little from him in the last week. The few texts that she had received were sweet but short. The phone calls were hurried and brief. Praying that God would watch closely over Jace, she turned back to her current project.

Mibs added the finishing touches on her new window display – a theme of vintage sewing items. Retro and vintage clothing seemed to be in style this season, and she'd decided to highlight those types of patterns and various materials as this month's specials. Two mannequins featured eye-catching creations. One was dressed in a vintage blue-and-white-striped, combed cotton sundress. The second wore a navy cap-sleeve pencil dress. Propped in front of the dresses were the patterns used to create them, and arranged around the two mannequins were era sewing items. Centered in the window was a vintage Singer Feather Light portable sewing machine, complete with a faded, light green carrying box and an old book titled *Student Manual of Machine Sewing*. A hand-crocheted lace tablecloth was spread on the left side of the window shelf. Exhibited on its surface were a Mason jar filled with old spools of thread, a scattering of small, wooden needle cylinders, vintage buttons still on their cardboard holders, and a half-dozen tatting shuttles with several yards of delicate, tatted lace meandering around the items. The opposite side of the window showcased a Fiestaware bowl heaped with an array of thimbles, including hand-painted, sterling silver, and wooden. Strategically placed nearby was a set of embroidered, bluebird, day-of-the-week kitchen dish towels.

After placing the bowl of thimbles – the last item planned for the display – Mibs stepped back and surveyed her work. "Not bad," she complimented herself out loud. "Of course, I wouldn't have some of these great items if I hadn't stopped at Tony's place."

Calling to mind the trip to Tony's Vintage Treasures and Fix-it Shop, Mibs fondly thought about her former classmate. She had gone to Tony's on three other occasions. One time she had stopped to have some older sewing machines checked and oiled, another time to wander around, and a third visit was with Jace to purchase a small bench for his mudroom. Each time, a cheerful young man barely past his teens had served her. His dark hair and features had reminded her of someone, but she was sure she had never met the young man before. Yesterday when she entered the resale and fix-it store, she realized why he seemed familiar. Mibs saw the clerk stationed by the counter, and beside him, she noticed a taller, slightly older man with similar hair, eyes, and complexion.

Hesitating in the middle of the aisle, Mibs took a second glance at the brown-eyed man with coal-black hair unwrapping antique porcelain insulators and setting them on the counter. "Tony!" she said in surprise.

He turned toward her at the sound of his name. His eyes came to life, and he smiled. "Mirabelle Monahan! What a wonderful surprise to see you."

He came from behind the counter, and Anthony Vitali greeted her, grabbing both of her hands. "Mibs! *Mon cher ami.* It has been a long time."

A wave of happiness swept through Mibs as she gazed up at the man who had been her friend since childhood. It had been over five years since she last saw him. Long enough for the slim, cute boy to turn into an incredibly handsome man.

His chocolate-brown eyes, framed by long, black lashes, seemed to have even more depth than she remembered. A couple small wrinkles were barely noticeable, giving him a note of maturity. But there was an intensity in his gaze that she didn't recognize. Gone was the shattered sadness that she had seen the last time they had spoken.

Mibs considered the hands that held hers. She remembered the long, slender fingers, which could play the piano with expertise, use a computer with proficiency, or repair just about anything they touched. Her thoughts drifted to the day when things had changed drastically.

It was the day his talented hands were turned into tight fists, only his self-control apparently stopping them from punching anything and anyone around him. The day that many of those he had considered friends turned against him.

~~

It was the last month of his senior year and Mibs' junior year. Tony's father, an accountant, had been arrested and charged with felony embezzlement. Roberto Vitali's picture was in the paper, front page, above the fold. It showed him being led away in handcuffs. The article stated that he stole money from his employer's company, Rittman Investments. Even though he pleaded innocent, he had been found guilty and sentenced to a 250,000 dollar fine and ten years in jail. They had lost their home, car, everything they owned, and Tony had lost his father he respected and loved.

Mibs remembered the anger and hurt in his voice as he told everyone that his "father had been framed." And that his father "was an honest man and would never steal anything." Leisa Vitali, his mother, had died in a car accident when Anthony was eight. Suddenly, both his parents were gone, and he was alone.

Those last few weeks before graduation had been rough on Tony. There were whispers behind his back; many students had stopped talking when he walked up, and some of them even called his dad *a thief* to his face. Mibs found it hard to understand how people could be so cruel. Her heart had ached for him.

Tony and Mibs had been friends since they met in summer bible school when she was in third grade. It wasn't until middle school that she and Tony realized they considered each other more than just friends. Living in the same neighborhood and going to the same school often meant spending many hours together. When Tony had needed a motherly shoulder to lean on, he'd visit Aunt Bernie. Roberto Vitali would occasionally step in when Mibs needed a male role model. Mr. Vitali had even been her escort to the seventh-grade father-daughter dance. They weren't born into the same family, but Tony and Mibs were brother and sister in every other sense.

Mibs recalled that during the last few weeks of school, Tony had stayed at his cousin's house. She knew that because of his outstanding grades, he had offers of scholarships at several universities. He'd told her his original plan – to go to a nearby college and commute from home. But after his father's incarceration, he changed his mind and headed to an excellent university in another state. Mibs heard that two years after Tony had started college, Roberto Vitali died in prison from a heart attack. She had written to Tony, but her letters went unanswered. Mibs surmised that Tony wanted to avoid memories of his hometown while he worked on his college degree. But they still exchanged Christmas cards, so he hadn't cut himself completely off from her.

~~

"Tony, I didn't know you were back in town!" Mibs exclaimed. "Then, does that mean..." She waved her uplifted arm around the room. "This is your place?"

He folded his arms across his chest—obviously proud of his business—and Anthony Vitali nodded. "Yes, it's one of my means of income."

Raising her eyebrows and nodding, Mibs responded, "*One* of your means of income. Really?" She thought about asking him what other businesses he had, but instead, she threw her arms around him and hugged him. "Oh, Tony! It's so good to see you."

The two friends held their embrace for a moment before pulling away. "Mibs," Tony said, "you are one of the few people I missed from Havendale." He indicated two chairs next to the counter, and they sat down. "How have you been? I saw that you opened a sewing shop. I drove by one evening, but you had already closed for the day."

As Mibs described her sewing business and the decision to forgo working on her master's degree, Tony listened attentively.

"I heard that you had given up your dream to be a fashion designer to come home and take care of Aunt Bernie. How is she?"

"Oh! Who told you that?" Mibs questioned,

embarrassed that the comment made her decision sound altruistic, assuring herself that she had made the right decision. "I'm glad we opened Monahan's Sewing Shop. And Aunt Bernie is doing well."

"I've known you long enough to know that you think of others first."

As they visited for the next half-hour, Tony explained that he didn't live in Havendale and drove the 45 miles here once or twice a week. His cousin, Leo, with the help of his son, Luca, ran the shop. He enjoyed coming here and repairing items that didn't work correctly but let Leo and Luca run the store's daily activities. His current project was fixing a grandfather clock that he'd purchased at an estate sale. He loved going to auctions and estate sales. However, his primary income came from being a computer specialist. His apparent natural ability to understand the technological intricacies surrounding computers and electronics had been good when he was a teenager. After attending a university considered one of the best in the country for those specializing in IT degrees, Tony had honed his abilities and acquired knowledge that made him a highly sought-after expert in the field. In what little time left after that, he gave free piano lessons at his local community center to underprivileged kids, something he did for his own pleasure. He also gave piano lessons to well-to-do students, something he did for lucrative fees.

Mibs was happy that he had built a good life for himself. She only wished that his father had lived long enough to see what a genuinely good man Tony had become. It was heart-wrenchingly sad to know that Roberto Vitali had died before the documents containing the proof of his innocence had been found. The local newspapers didn't say how the records were discovered or how they ended up on the district attorney's desk. Apparently, the real embezzler had been Gregory Rittman himself. With his senior accountant's help, a man named Jonesburg, he had been skimming money that should have gone to the stockholders. When it became likely they might be caught, the computer accounts were falsified to implicate Vitali. It would've taken a talented computer analyst to uncover the altered versions.

Mibs would never ask, but she couldn't help wondering if the computer wizard who had revealed the truth sat across from her now. Her chest swelled with admiration as she gazed at her childhood friend.

~~

Since he was nine years old, Anthony Vitali had thought of Mirabelle Monahan as a good friend and confidante. Tony was pleased to realize Mibs had grown into a gracious and attractive woman. Her hair reminded him of strawberries and cream. Her eyes sparkled with energy. Her smile radiated sincere happiness. When did his childhood chum become such a beautiful woman? Tony tapped Mibs on the shoulder.

"Since you didn't know I was the 'Tony' who owned this place, you didn't come in to visit. Was there something you were searching for?" He contemplated the face of the young woman sitting beside him. *What does she want...really want?*

She answered his question with a bright smile. "I came on a scavenger hunt for classic sewing items." Jumping up and heading to the front of the store, Mibs motioned for Tony to follow. "I want to start with that Feather Light sewing machine if you still have it. I noticed it the last time I was here."

The energy that emanated from the enthusiastic girl was infectious. Anthony Vitali found himself smiling as he followed her through the familiar aisles stacked with a hodgepodge of items. By the time Mirabelle had collected an array of sewing memorabilia and deposited everything on the counter, Tony laughed.

Luca, the young assistant Mibs had met on previous visits, rang up the purchases. Tony had stepped away but returned shortly with a pristine, daffodil-colored Fiestaware bowl. "You mentioned trying to decide what to use to display your collection of thimbles. Would this be a good choice?"

"That would be *perfect!*" Her eyes lit up with pleasure. Carefully taking the bowl from Tony, she placed it on the counter. "Please, ring this up, too, Luca."

Tony shook his head. "No, don't add it to the bill." He gazed at his friend. He placed his hand on her shoulder. "This is something I want to give you."

Her mouth opened and closed a couple times before she softly responded, "Tony, I don't know what to say."

Pulling a sheet of tissue paper from the stack on the counter, Tony picked up the bowl and began carefully wrapping it. "Say, 'thank you'." He winked, then handed the wrapped package to Luca.

Tony helped Mibs carry her purchases to her car and stored them in the trunk. "When do you plan on having your window display done? I'll come by and see how it turned out."

"It should only take a few days," she answered, "hopefully by Friday." The wind began to pick up, and Mibs reached up to tuck away the strands of hair the breeze had blown across her face. "I'd better head back to the shop and get these things inside before it starts raining."

"The weather report mentioned heavy rains during the next couple of days." Tony paused. "But it's supposed to clear up by Saturday and be sunny." He tilted his head as he studied Mirabelle. "I'm planning on going to an auction on Saturday. I'd like it if you'd come with me."

"Oh." Mibs hesitated. "I enjoy going to auctions, but...I don't know."

"You don't know?" Tony questioned. "How about if I sweeten the deal and take you out to dinner after?"

With a quick breath, Mibs responded, "Well, I've been dating someone. I don't know if he will be in town this weekend."

"Ah! You've got a boyfriend," he restated. He reached over and lifted the hair that had blown across her face again and tucked it behind her ear. "Hmm, what's his name? Maybe he would like to come too."

Mibs shrugged her shoulders. "His name is Jace Trueblood. He's a detective, and he's out of town right now working with another police department."

"Where is he working?" Tony asked. "When will he be back?"

Wrinkling her brow, Mibs answered, "I'm not sure exactly where he is or how long he'll be gone."

This brought a smirk to Tony's face. "You're dating this guy, but you don't know where he is and when he'll be back? Hmm."

"Don't say it like that!" Mibs lightly slugged her friend in the arm. "He's a great guy, and I like him."

Tony stepped back and held up his hands in surrender as his smirk turned into a smile. "Okay! I get it. You care about the guy." He rubbed his arm in exaggeration, and then he shook his head. "I'd forgotten how hard you could hit." Chuckling, he teased, "If he doesn't get back, and if I promise to watch what I say, would you come with me on Saturday? I'd love some company."

"It could be fun," Mibs conceded. "But I don't close the shop until one o'clock. What time is the auction?"

"It starts at eleven, but the items I'm interested in aren't likely to be bid on that early." Tony ran his hand across his chin. "It's only about a twenty-minute drive from here, but it might be easier if you could meet me there. That is if you decide to come."

Mibs stepped forward and gave Tony a quick hug. "If I'm not too tired after I close up and if Jace hasn't returned, I'll drive over."

"Good! Give me your number, and I'll text you the directions." After exchanging numbers, Tony waved and headed back to the store, exclaiming, "I hope you decide to come!"

Chapter 6

Jace continued to work with Sergeant McCormick and the Broadly police for over a week. He was in the bullpen at their station, strategizing with members of their narcotics unit about the information on the displayed crime board.

McCormick entered the area and strolled up to the assembled group. He was accompanied by a short, young-looking man.

"Detective Sergeant Trueblood," McCormick said, "I don't believe you've met Major Martin Fleming of the State Highway Patrol. He's head of a specialized drug prevention unit. He and some others are joining us during this operation."

Jace regarded the unit leader who, at first glance, could pass for someone in their early twenties. After a closer look, Jace noticed an attentiveness in the major's eyes and a calm, sturdy manner in his stance that hinted at years of experience. A glance at Fleming gave the appearance of a thin, lanky body. But a more careful scan revealed ropy arms with long cords of muscles. The collar-length hair, faded shirt, and worn leather vest hinted that he was probably more often dressed in clothes designated for undercover work rather than his state trooper's uniform.

Holding out his hand, Jace said, "Hello, Major Fleming."

Fleming shook Jace's hand. Then, turning back to McCormick, he said, "You're right, Mike. He may be just the person we need."

Focusing intently on Fleming and McCormick, Jace listened as they discussed his background and that he wasn't from the area. "I assume you have a reason for talkin' 'bout me as if I weren't here."

Fleming gave Jace another once-over before asking, "Detective Trueblood, how would you like to go undercover?"

Without hesitation, Jace gave a decisive nod. "If that's what's needed to stop these drug dealers and bring Willy's killers to justice, I'm ready."

A short time later, Jace was at a federal building, sitting at a table across from Fleming. The state police officer was sharing information gathered on the suspected leaders of the cocaine operation. The paperwork he'd pulled out and spread across the table was similar to what was on the police department's crime board. However, this was more extensive. There were details from several surrounding states. This drug syndicate covered more than the town of Broadly.

"We've been working with the DEA and the highway patrol from connecting states." Fleming pulled a manilla envelope out of the stack of papers. He opened the flap and poured out a set of the photos, enlargements of those taken by William McBride.

"I understand that a friend of yours was shot and killed getting these pictures." Fleming's expression showed a brief hint of sympathy. "Sorry about his death." He tapped the photos taken by Willy. "These pictures confirmed what we suspected, and who some of the players in the business might be, and the extent of their operation. We've been trying to obtain proof against several of these men. Now we have it." Fleming took a long swig from a bottle of water. He placed the bottle on the table, pulled out a piece of spearmint gum, and popped it into his mouth. He slid another folder across the table.

Jace opened the folder and scanned the enclosed photocopies. After a quick pass through the information, he started back at the front, carefully reading each page. "Okay," Jace said, "this file is about a suspected head of a drug-smuggling operation based near the Texas border." Jace lifted his eyes. "Is this guy—Nolan Lee—someone I'll be dealing with when I go undercover? Do we have a picture of him?" Jace squinted at Fleming when he noticed that the undercover specialist was smiling.

"The picture should be here in a few minutes. Lee is an out-of-town dealer who'll be sneaking into the area within the next couple of days." Fleming pushed his chair back and stood. "In the meantime, let's get you fitted for the right kind of clothes." He opened the door to the small room and signaled for a man waiting in the hallway. "Mr. Rinker, would you come in now?"

The portly, middle-aged man approached Jace. "Well?"

"Well, what?" Jace eyed the guy.

"You have to stand up if I'm going to get your measurements."

"Oh! For my undercover outfit." Jace stood. "Sure. But..." Jace glanced at Fleming. "If I'm going to wear somethin' similar to what y'all have on, I can just buy somethin' at a clothing recycle place."

Fleming replied, "You aren't going to be working in the area where I'll be assigned. We have something else in mind for you." Jace caught the slight pucker of the major's brow. "In fact, if something goes wrong with your cover, you might find yourself in an extremely dangerous situation."

Before anything else could be said, the door opened again. A uniformed officer stepped in and handed a new folder to Fleming. Then, he turned back around and walked out without a word.

"This is the picture, passport, and other IDs we've been waiting for." After checking the contents of the folder, Fleming handed it to Jace. "Nice to meet you, Mr. Lee."

Ah, now I get it. Jace stared at the driver's license and passport bearing his picture. Jace had been told that the photographs taken of him before entering this room would be used to construct fake IDs, but he hadn't expected this.   Staring back at him was the image showing him as Nolan Lee.

The tailor who had been waiting—a little less than patiently—cleared his throat. "I only have a certain amount of time to get your clothing together."

"Hold your horses," Jace muttered as he took another minute to study the fake identifications.   Tossing the folder onto the table, he motioned to him.   "Okay, Mr. Rinker."

After the tailor had the needed measurements, Jace asked, "So, what kind of outfit are you fixin' for Mr. Nolan Lee?"

Rinker peeked over the top of his glasses and continued to scribble in a notebook; the man sighed. "It isn't one outfit. You'll need three suits, six shirts and coordinating ties, and one tuxedo."

"A tuxedo?" Jace questioned. He shot his eyes over to Fleming. The man shrugged.

"I'm sure you noticed, according to the cover story, Nolan Lee likes expensive things, so he dresses well and spends money freely." Fleming crossed his arms against his chest. "These criminals are thorough; they may check your hotel room. The luggage and clothing need to fit the image of someone like Lee. They may even plant a bug in your room and tap your hotel phone, so you'll have to stay in character even when you're alone in your room." Fleming rubbed his hand across his chin. "We'll give you a number to call in case something unexpected comes up. It'll be staffed 24-7 with trained officers. Assume that they'll be listening if you call, so you'll have to talk in code about what you need. But don't worry, our people are used to catching the gist of the request, even if you can't state it outright."

Jace furrowed his brow. "Sounds challenging, but I'll help y'all git it done."

"Humph," the tailor interrupted. "What size shoe do you wear, Mr. Truebl...I mean, Mr. Lee? I see that you're supposed to get a pair of expensive-looking boots and a pair of patent-leather oxford shoes." Then, turning to scowl at Major Fleming, he grumbled, "And you expect me to have everything ready in three days?"

After Jace gave him the information, Rinker slapped his folder shut, shook his head, and left the room.

Fleming pulled his chair out and motioned to Jace. "Sit down. Let's get started on your cover story. Starting now, until this operation is over, you *are* Nolan Lee. You answer only to that name. You learn everything in your cover story. You will walk like he would, act like he would, and think like he would." Fleming paused. "Do you understand, Detective Trueblood?"

Staring back, Jace said, "My name is Lee. Nolan Lee."

Chapter 7

Her niece leaned over the counter and called to her. "Aunt Bernie, do you have time to check out the window display I just finished?"

Bernice stepped carefully as she came from the back area to join her niece. She moved a bit better today, leaning less heavily on her cane. She had recovered well after her hip surgery; however, Bernice knew that Mibs was still concerned that she was doing too much. She was grateful that several people answered their 'help wanted' ad in the local paper and the community section of the town's website. Bernice now anxiously waited for the interviews to start.

The two Monahan ladies strolled side-by-side to the large, open window area.

"Oh, Mibs, the display is terrific! It's eye-catching!" Despite redirecting her life to become a shop owner instead of a master's degree student, Mibs seemed very happy.

As her niece stepped back, she tilted her head and stared, then she leaned in and adjusted a piece of fabric on the display. "There, that's much better."

It was apparent to Bernice that Mibs loved the unending diversity of colors and textures of the fabrics she worked with and handled each day. Mibs had shared with her that it bolstered her sense of creativity when those fabrics turned into something beautiful, something that made the customer feel good when they wore their specially-made item.

The ladies turned when they heard the door open, followed by the call of a cheery voice.

"Hello." A tall, robust woman scanned the store as she stepped up to the counter. She turned when Mibs answered her greeting.

~~

"Good afternoon." Mibs walked with Aunt Bernie back over to the counter and addressed the lady. "How may I help you?"

A pleasant smile radiated across her face. "I'm here for a job interview. My name is Deanna Maxwell."

"Oh, yes, Mrs. Maxwell. I'm Mibs Monahan. I'll be interviewing you today." Turning, she indicated her aunt. "This is Bernice Monahan." Mibs pointed to a table and chairs in a far corner. "Please come over and sit down."

Contemplating the first applicant of the day, she judged her to be in the mid-forties. Physical attributes included a sturdy build, ruddy complexion, and gray-streaked brown hair, none of which stood out noticeably compared to the friendly grin and sparkling eyes that dominated her features.

Mibs had called three women and one man out of the eight people who had applied for the job.

After talking to Deanna Maxwell for a while, Mibs learned that she wanted to work only part-time during the days when her three kids were in school. Mibs also found out that Mrs. Maxwell had been a full-time homemaker for years. Some previous activities included being treasurer for the PTA, coordinator, designer of costumes for high school plays, and town chairperson for the local girl scout troops.

Despite the limited availability, Mibs liked her personality and background enough to proceed to the next part of the interview: a money handling review and a sewing challenge. Retrieving a cash drawer from a nearby shelf, she slid it in front of Deanna. "Please count down this drawer and let me know how much money it contains."

Eyeing Mibs for half a beat, Deanna nodded, then started with the pennies. She counted down the drawer competently. "Fifty dollars and thirty-five cents," Deanna stated with assurance. She also did an excellent job demonstrating her sewing ability by reattaching a missing button and neatly repairing a tear along the seam of a work shirt.

Mibs made sure she had Deanna's contact information before the woman left, promising that she would let her know the decision within a couple of days.

The following two interviews were conducted without interruption. Aunt Bernie had waited on the few clients who needed help while Mibs talked to applicants. The fourth and final person to be interviewed walked in at a moment when several customers were already in the shop hunting for material and sewing items.

The young lady, petite, black-haired, and with almond-shaped dark eyes, entered and waited patiently for her turn.

Mibs greeted her. "I'll be with you as soon as I can. You're welcome to check things out or sit down if you prefer."

It took Mibs almost twenty minutes to meet the customers' needs. As her aunt finished the sale for the last buyer, Mibs scanned the shop, locating the composed and quiet woman paging through a pattern book. "Hi. Mary Wong?"

"Yes," Mary answered as she stood and followed Mibs to the interview area.

"Would you prefer that I call you Miss Wong or Mary?" Mibs queried.

"Mary, please," she politely responded.

By the time the last interview was finished, the final customer had been waited on, and the door was locked for the day, Aunt Bernie and Mibs were both ready to relax.

Aunt Bernie heated water for a pot of tea, warmed up soup, and made sandwiches while Mibs completed the routine for closing the shop. Collapsing with a sigh onto a chair, Mibs leaned over and inhaled the enticing aroma of the broccoli cheese soup.

"It smells wonderful," Mibs declared. After saying a quick prayer of thanksgiving for their meal, Mibs picked up a soup spoon and savored the first bite. "I'm glad you made sandwiches, too. I'm ready to eat just about anything you put in front of me." Mibs realized that being on her feet much of the day, hefting containers of stock, and wrestling around bolts of material, kept her in good shape. Her job's physical activity was like being in an all-day gym, not only building muscle but also giving her a hearty appetite.

"Thank you, Aunt Bernie, for putting dinner together." She reached over and placed one meat, cheese, lettuce, and tomato sandwich on her dish. She sighed before taking a bite. "Tomorrow, I'll put something in the crockpot and have a hot meal ready for us at the end of the day."

Both women ate silently for ten minutes before Aunt Bernie asked, "Well, what did you think about the applicants? Do you think you may hire one of them?" She pushed her empty bowl aside and pulled her sandwich closer as she waited for Mibs to swallow a sip of tea.

"I think I'll hire more than one," Mibs declared. "The two people I think will work the best for us both want part-time jobs. Fortunately, the hours they're seeking balance out well with what we need. Deanna Maxwell can work from nine until two weekdays. Mary Wong is a college student and wants to work a few hours in the afternoons and Saturday mornings. They both have wonderful personalities, quite different, but genuinely nice. And they both seem to be able to handle money as well as use a needle and thread."

Taking a couple minutes to enjoy a bite of her sandwich before continuing, Mibs paused. "Deanna has experience not only sewing for her family but also making outfits for the high school drama club. Mary's stitches on a skirt I handed to her were so small and precise that they were barely noticeable. I think that I'll call them in the morning and offer each a job."

"Good." Aunt Bernie said, relief obvious in her tone and reflection.

Aunt Bernie had been slowing down recently, and even though Mibs had an abundance of energy, there was only so much one person could do.

"I'm anxious to get to know them. Did the women say when they can start?"

Mibs set her napkin on the empty plate, and leaned back in her chair. "They both indicated that they could start right away. I think I'll call tomorrow morning and ask them to come on Monday." Pushing herself away from the table, she stacked the dishes and utensils. "How about a dish of ice cream for dessert?" Before her aunt could answer, her cell phone rang. Mibs recognized the notes of the song, "You Are My Sunshine," which she had programmed for Jace's number.

A combination of relief and joy surged through her. Mibs hadn't heard from Jace for longer than she liked. Worry had begun to gnaw its way into her thoughts. "Jace! Hi! How are you?"

"Hello, Mibs." He sounded exhausted. "I'm

okay. Sorry I haven't called for several days. Things have been hectic, reaching a critical point. I ended up going undercover, and I'm only able to call you when I'm in a specified secure location. If I'm anywhere other than this safe house, I have to keep the appearance and voice of the character I'm supposed to be."

"As long as you're okay." Mibs began to pace across the room. "You hadn't mentioned that you would be doing undercover work. Isn't that dangerous?"

"Sergeant McCormick, the detective from Broadly Police, reviewed my background and decided that I could handle the job. He also considered that I was less likely to be recognized than someone from the local police force.

"Oh, honey, please be careful!" Mibs implored.

"I plan on treading carefully. Hey, don't worry too much, Mibs. I have a lot of backup officers. This drug ring covers several states, so federal officers are involved, too. Since the parameter includes places near our area, Lieutenant Taylor has agreed to lend me to the combined agencies task force for the time being."

"Do you have any idea how long you will be gone, Jace?"

"I'm sorry, Mibs. I hope it won't be too long, but there is no way of knowing how many days this may take."

Mibs' voice trembled as she tried to calm her

nerves. "I...understand. I just wish the job were finished and you were already home."

"Believe me, darlin', I wish I was there with you right now." Jace's words made Mibs miss him even more. "I've been dreamin' of how good it would be to hold you in my arms even for a minute."

"Mm, that sounds like a nice dream," murmured Mibs.

"Sweetheart." Jace sighed. "Sorry. I have to go."

"You're working tonight?"

"Just sharing information and doing paperwork," Jace explained. "It will be late when I'm done, so I'm just going back to the hotel and, hopefully, get a little sleep." Mibs heard what sounded like a yawn echo over the phone. "Tomorrow's Saturday, isn't it? How about I call after you close up tomorrow, and we can talk again. Now, don't worry if something comes up and I can't call. I have to leave my phone here, but I will try to slip over for a few minutes."

"That would be nice." Happiness at the idea of hearing his voice again, even if it was just on the phone, slipped into Mibs' heart. She suddenly remembered her promise to Tony. "Oh, wait...Saturday, I told a friend that I might meet him after the shop closed."

"Oh, okay," Jace replied, his voice hesitant with disappointment. "How 'bout I try callin' you later Saturday night?"

"No," Mibs started to say.

"No?" Jace interrupted. "Now you got me wondering about the 'him' you plan to meet."

"I didn't mean *no*, don't call." Mibs took a deep breath. "I mean no, you don't have to wait. Call me if you can in the afternoon. I'll wait here. I'll text Tony and tell him I can't make it."

"Thank you, Mibs," Jace responded, "but I don't want you to cancel on your friend. Go meet him." Mibs heard the uncertainty in her boyfriend's voice. "Do I know this guy?"

"I doubt you do." Mibs paced, wishing Jace was home already. "Tony's a long-time friend. Someone I went to school with. He grew up in my neighborhood."

"I'll have to meet him sometime." Jace stopped talking for a moment; another voice could be heard in the background. "Mibs, I have to go. I'll call you tomorrow, late evening if I can."

"All right," Mibs said. "I'll be waiting."

"Got to go. Bye, Mibs." The line went dead.

"Is everything all right?" Aunt Bernie queried.

Mibs nodded, but she couldn't hide the disappointment in her voice. "Jace is okay. I just wanted to talk to him longer." Sighing, she walked over and picked up the dishes she had stacked a few minutes earlier. "Let me set these aside; then I'll tell you what he said."

Two hours later, Mibs had finished sweeping, mopping, and dusting her apartment. She had kicked off her shoes and plopped down on the sofa. After surfing the television stations for several minutes, she turned it off and picked up a book. The phone rang before she finished the first page.

"Hello, Jace?" She didn't take time to let her mind register that it wasn't the tone for Jace's number. "Did you get another chance to call?"

"No, sorry to disappoint you. It's Tony," Anthony corrected. "Mibs, do you want me to phone later? It sounds like you're waiting for a call."

"Please don't hang up, Tony," Mibs reassured him. "How's it going? Are you ready for the auction?"

"I'm still planning on being there, but I thought I'd check to see if you think you may come after you close tomorrow. If you do, I'll take you to an early dinner afterward. I know a place that has exceptional *calzones* and fresh garden salads. The *calzones* are loaded with pepperoni, mushrooms, gooey cheese, and wonderful fresh basil. I think you'll love them."

"That sounds good! Unless something unexpected comes up, I should be there between 1:20 and 1:30. Will the auction still be going on that late?"

"It'll probably last until around four o'clock. The auctioneer will go through the big items earlier in the day, mostly furniture. I stopped this afternoon and checked out the different things stacked on trailers and the other items displayed. I have my eye on a couple smaller antiques that were dispersed among boxes of odds and ends. I may have to buy whole boxes of knickknacks to get the pieces I want," Tony explained. "But that's part of the fun of auctions. Were the directions I texted clear enough?"

"Yes. I shouldn't have any trouble getting there." Mibs' mood lifted, and she was excited about going. She hadn't been to an auction in a long time. "I'm glad the weather is supposed to clear up. The forecast still predicts a nice day tomorrow."

"Sounds like it will be. Hey, do you want me to grab a bidding card for you when I pick up one for myself? Maybe there'll be something that catches your attention you'll want to bid on."

"Ah, I guess. Does it matter if you get one and I don't use it?"

"Not at all; it happens all the time," Tony said. "I'll try to be near the auction truck so you can find me. Glad you're coming, Mirabelle. See you tomorrow, *mon cher ami*."

"Goodnight. See you tomorrow."

After talking to Tony, Mibs texted Aunt Bernie that she would be heading to the country after work. She picked up the book she had set aside, *The Harvester* by Gene Stratton Porter, and leaned back and began to relax.

Chapter 8

The next morning, as Mibs lifted the pressure foot on her sewing machine and moved the material forward, she smiled and recalled the agitated girl who had come in three days before. A young woman had opened the door to Monahan's and had rushed in. The girl had dashed toward Mibs, dumped a lavender-colored, full-length dress onto her lap, and had demanded, "You have to help me!"

Mibs had grabbed the outfit before it slid off her lap, and considered the frazzled customer. "What kind of help do you need?"

"My brother's wedding is in eight days. I'm a bridesmaid, and I have to wear this dress, and it doesn't fit anymore. It was a little tight when we bought it, and I wanted it to be nice for the wedding, so I went on a crash diet."

Mibs had pushed the chair back and stood. "Is it still too tight?"

"No!" the young woman had moaned. "It's too big now! I lost over fifteen pounds, and now it's worse than when it was a bit tight."

Mibs had taken a deep breath, forced herself to swallow the laugh that threatened to erupt from her throat, then had gestured for the girl to come to the dressing area in the back of the shop. "Why don't you put the dress on and let me see what we can do?"

While the soon-to-be bridesmaid had slipped

on the troublesome gown, Mibs had gone to the front of the store and stepped behind the counter. In the small kitchenette area, she set a peppermint tea bag into a ceramic mug and filled it with steaming water from the hot water dispenser. She placed the cup on a tray along with a sugar container and spoon, then carried them back with her. When the girl had emerged, Mibs had her complete a full turn as she critiqued the garment.

The silky, flowing outfit hung loosely in several places, the waistline hit lower than it should on the girl's short frame, and the light purple was not a complementary shade for the wearer's complexion. Mibs had clamped her mouth shut as she tried to think of subtle ways to talk about the unflattering outfit.

"I don't believe you told me your name. I'm Mibs Monahan."

"My name is Anna Zimmerman," the lavender-material-encased girl had said, "and I know who you are because you made some outfits for my aunt, Mary Miner. I believe you're the one who made that gorgeous baby blanket for her, too."

"Oh, yes, of course. Ms. Miner is a nice lady." Taking time to consider the alterations needed for the dress, Mibs had crossed her arms. "Hmm, let me grab my sewing box." She pointed to the tray. "Would you like a cup of tea? I find peppermint often helps me when I'm distracted with a problem."

The woman hadn't responded.

Mibs had returned with the container that held her sewing tools. She had draped a measuring tape around her neck and pulled out a notepad. "Now, let's take some measurements."

Anna had stared at the hem and shook her head. "This didn't seem as long when it fit tighter." She frowned. "I wish Chelsea would have chosen a different color."

"I wondered about that," Mibs had commented. "This isn't a shade that you would have chosen, is it?"

Anna had rolled her eyes and choked out, "Of course not!" Sighing, she conceded, "But it *is* Chelsea's wedding, and she should have what she wants."

"Anna, are there other bridesmaids?"

"Yes. Two others. Why are you asking?"

Mibs had tapped her chin. "Do all of you have exactly the same bridesmaid's dresses?"

"The same color, but the styles are each slightly different." Anna scrunched her face.

"So...lavender is the only wedding color the bride is using?"

Anna had shrugged her shoulders, which caused Mibs to lose the spot across the girl's back where she'd been measuring. "Her colors are lavender and black. At first, I thought that was an odd combination. After seeing some of the decorations, I decided that they are nice together." Holding her arms out from her sides, she had said, "Except on me!"

Mibs had grabbed the girl's shoulders and

straightened the girl's posture. "You have to hold still, Anna, if you want me to jot down the measurements correctly." After writing down numbers in her notebook, Mibs had said, "What if we added a touch of black to this dress?"

"What?" Anna's forehead had wrinkled.

"If we lowered this high neckline a little, gave it more of a sweetheart cut, I could add a thin border of black silk along the edge. We could also add narrow black piping around the waistline when I move it up several inches." Quickly drawing a sketch on her notepad, Mibs showed Anna what she had in mind. "It would still have the matching lavender color, but the black trim would present the slightest break in the pale shade. You could add stylish black jewelry."

"Oh...my," Anna had mumbled as she scanned the drawing, "that would be so much nicer."

"I think that touch of difference would work a lot better with your complexion and your figure."

Anna had seemed to consider the suggestions.

"Do you think the bride would mind?"

Anna had paused. A smile slowly formed on her lips. "All she asked was that we wear this same purple shade," she commented. She bobbed her head. "Let's do it!" She reached for the cup of tea but suddenly stopped. "Wait. Will you be able to get it done by next week?"

Mibs had chuckled. "I can if you stand still long enough for me to get your measurements."

Getting up early Saturday allowed Mibs to work without interruption on Anna's dress. The hardest part, changing the neckline, was almost finished. She sat back from her sewing machine and picked up her needle and thread. Then Mibs started tacking down the inside lining.

"My goodness! What time did you get up, my dear girl?" Aunt Bernie moved well this morning with just a little help from her cane, one of her good days. "Have you had breakfast?"

Shrugging, Mibs said, "I just had coffee. Getting started on this dress seemed more important than eating." She tied off the end of the lavender thread and reached for her scissors and snipped the ends.

"Pish posh," Aunt Bernie uttered. "How many times have I explained that breakfast is an important meal?" Without further words, she picked up Mibs' phone and tapped in a familiar number. "Good morning, Hazel. Are you still at the bakery?" She listened for a moment, then responded, "You're correct; I would like you to pop over with some baked goods. How about two cranberry-orange muffins and two pecan Danishes?"

Mibs could hear Hazel's voice over the phone. "I wouldn't mind at all, Bernie. Be there in a jiff."

After placing her request with Hazel, Aunt Bernie gave Mibs one of her motherly hugs. "Muffins aren't the perfect breakfast, but they're better than nothing. I'll go get you a glass of orange juice and put on a fresh pot of coffee."

Mibs smiled and shook her head as she watched her aunt return to the kitchenette. Love and admiration filled her heart for the woman who had raised her. She took a deep breath and exhaled, then turned back to her work.

By the time Monahan's opened at nine, the alterations on Anna Zimmerman's dress were completed. Mibs expected the coordinator from the local theater group between nine and nine-thirty. Mrs. Barns planned on bringing a list of new costumes that they were requesting for a children's play scheduled for the end of summer, just before school reopened. Mibs would meet the young aspiring actors next Thursday to take measurements and obtain needed details for the clothing desired for a modern production of *The Wizard of Oz*.

The two new employees whom Mibs had contacted that morning both seemed eager to start on Monday. Once their training was completed, Deanna would work Monday through Friday from nine to two. Mary would work Tuesday through Friday from 1:15 to 5:15 and also on Saturday mornings. The new employees would be a great help with constructing the theater's costumes.

Usually, Mibs welcomed a consistent flow of customers, but today she silently wished for a slow day, in the hope that she could head out of town a few minutes after closing. She hung up the bridesmaid dress and started back to the counter when the door opened. The jingle of the overhead bells became drowned out by the hearty welcome coming from Mrs. Barns as she scurried into the dressmaker's shop.

"Good morning! Good morning to the Monahans!" The enthusiastic woman plopped a thick, well-worn binder on the counter.

"Hello, Mrs. Barns." Mibs reached under the counter and pulled out her sketch pad and pencils. "How are you this fine day?" She noticed that the woman had added new blond highlights to her hair. The usual pumpkin-colored nail polish had been replaced by a sparkly pink shade.

Clasping her hands together, the bubbly play coordinator inhaled a deep breath before booming out her reply. "I'm doing wonderful, simply wonderful. We have a fantastic group of junior thespians eager to begin working on the play." Opening her folder, she showed pictures of costumes used in previous versions of the *Wizard of Oz*. "Do you think you can make outfits similar to these?"

Mibs suggested that their discussion move to a nearby table to examine the samples more closely, take notes, and make plans.

An hour later, Mibs escorted Mrs. Barns to the door, assuring her that work on the costumes would begin by the end of next week.

While working with Mrs. Barns, Mibs had noted the two customers who came in, both greeted and helped by Aunt Bernie. After the coordinator left, Mibs took a few minutes to get another cup of coffee and the last muffin, then sat down behind the counter next to her aunt.

"Well, how was the meeting with the theater lady?" Aunt Bernie turned toward Mibs, head tilted in curiosity.

"Better than I anticipated." Mibs took a big bite of muffin, enjoying the orange and cranberry blend of flavors. After swallowing, she explained that they had fewer costumes to construct than she had initially thought Mrs. Barns would want. "I'm anxious to get the kids' measurements because I can't order the needed material until I know how many yards of each fabric will be required." Eagerly Mibs stated, "I think it will be fun making these outfits. Maybe we can even go to the play when it opens."

The Monahan ladies turned to the door when it opened again. Three young girls entered. Mibs estimated their ages to be between eleven and thirteen; the term "tweens" came to mind.

The trio moved in unison, taking tentative steps as they slowly approached the counter. Mibs and Bernie smiled at each other. It wasn't the first time they had dealt with tweens. Occasionally, someone between the ages of six and sixteen would come in seeking help, usually for a school or club project.

"Hi." Mibs placed her elbows on the spacious counter and rested her chin on clasped fingers, putting herself at eye level with the girls. "What do you need today, ladies?"

A sweetly gamine-faced blonde with long hair and crystal-blue eyes glanced back at her friends before clearing her throat. "Hi, um...my name is Georgia; this is Margot and Kassidy. Um...I saw an ad that said you gave sewing lessons. Would you also give lessons on doing embroidery?" Pulling a plastic bag from behind her back, she released a heavy sigh before opening it and removing a dresser scarf.

Mibs sat back as the girl placed the scarf in front of her. The cloth streaked with purple stains was damp from an apparent attempt to wash out the offending blotches. The cleaning effort only managed to make it worse, the color spreading and dyeing the cotton material. Despite the stains, the detailed design was easily visible. Leaves, flowers, and birds flowed through the piece, which would have graced the top of a dresser or buffet.

"It was an accident," Margot, the brown-haired pre-teen standing closest to the one who had spoken first, said in a soft voice.

"We were dancing and bumped the container of juice." A mien of regret etched the dark, worried face of the pretty, young Kassidy.

"Accidents happen." Aunt Bernie sympathized with the fretting group of girls. "If I understand what you are asking, the three of you want to make a new dresser scarf to replace the one that was stained. Correct?"

Three heads nodded in unison. Georgia, who seemed to be the spokesperson for the group, responded, "Yes, we would like to try. This scarf belongs to my grandmother. It's something she made when she was a girl, just a few years younger than I am now." Puckering her mouth, she bowed her head in a forlorn gesture. "Do you think we can do it, make something that is just like this one?"

"I don't see why not," Mibs empathized, "as long as the three of you are willing to work together and put in the time." Pausing, Mibs realized that time was at a premium right now. "There is one problem. I don't know if I can fit anything more into the current schedule. When do you hope to have this project completed?"

"As soon as possible," Margot and Kassidy replied at the same time.

"Hmm." Aunt Bernie stared at the girls. "Your grandmother doesn't know about this. Does she?"

Georgia slowly shook her head. "No, we're hoping we can get it replaced before she finds out." Guilty eyes peeked up from half-closed lids.

Mibs hadn't considered the possibility that

this was a secret mission that the girls hoped to complete without disappointing the grandmother. Surreptitiously glancing at her aunt, she tried to suppress a grin. These girls weren't any better at hiding information from Aunt Bernie than she had been as a child.

"Do you girls have any free time after school or on Saturdays?" her aunt asked.

Georgia, Margot, and Kassidy all nodded, then stood quietly, waiting with anxious expressions.

"Mibs, can you prepare a new piece of material and sketch this design on it, so the girls can start working next week?" Aunt Bernie requested, not waiting for an answer. Then, turning back and addressing the potential needle-work students, Aunt Bernie made an offer. "Mibs does not have the time currently to help teach you these embroidery stitches, but I do. However, you girls will have to do the bulk of the stitching. Teaching these various stitches and giving guidance to each of you as you learn them is the most these old hands will be able to do. But your young fingers should be able to complete the task without much trouble."

By the time the group left, Aunt Bernie had convinced the young ladies that it would be best to talk to Georgia's grandmother, be upfront about what had happened, and explain how they were trying to make it right.

"Before I dry this dresser scarf and begin recreating the design, I'm going to soak it in some vinegar and liquid detergent with cold water. I think a lot of the stain may still come out. I can also sponge it with rubbing alcohol. That may help, too." Mibs held the embroidered piece up to the light. "Maybe we should have suggested to the girls the possibility of getting a majority of the stain out before they made plans to make a completely new one," she suggested to her aunt.

Aunt Bernie squinted and shook her head. "Definitely not. These girls are at an age when they need to learn to take responsibility for their actions, even accidents. I think it's admirable that kids this age want to do the right thing. Besides..." The elderly woman folded her hands primly in her lap. "Then they would likely never learn to embroider, a skill they may appreciate someday." Aunt Bernie patted Mibs' hand. "You should try to minimize the stains on the scarf, but wait until they finish the new one before you give this one back."

Chapter 9

By 12:30, Mibs had finished a chef salad while Aunt Bernie sat behind the counter, available if any last-minute customers came in. After devouring her lunch, Mibs traded places with her aunt. While Aunt Bernie had a bite to eat, Mibs counted down the cash drawer and began the closing tasks. By 1:05 p.m., she had kissed her aunt on the cheek and hurried to her car. Eighteen minutes later, eager to join the excitement of the auction that seemed to be still going strong, she pulled onto a mowed field doubling as a parking lot.

Mibs meandered through the throng of auction attendees, searching for Anthony Vitali. As she neared the auctioneer's truck, she saw a bright blue cap waving above the nearby heads. Tony had been watching for her. His six-foot-one stature made it easy for Mibs to pick him out of the crowd. She threaded her way toward him; he met her halfway, settling the hat back on his dark, wavy hair.

"Mirabelle Monahan, I'm glad to see you came."

Mibs felt welcomed by Tony's dazzling smile.

"Did you have any trouble finding the place?"

Mibs accepted his offered hand as he led her back to his spot. "Not at all. The directions were clear. Have you bid on the items you wanted yet?"

"Some. I already have the back seat of my pick-up half full of great finds. There are a couple things that should be coming up for bid in a few minutes." He handed Mibs a rectangular card approximately three by seven inches with the number 189 stamped in large, bold print on one side. He guided her closer to the open-window, covered-bed truck. "Here's a card in case you want to bid on anything." He held a second card and reminded her that she merely had to hold up her numbered card if she wanted to bid. He demonstrated the technique by raising his card to head height, then realized that the auctioneer had started selling the next item, and he had just unwittingly made a bid. "Whoops! I wonder what I just bid on and how much it was." Fortunately, someone placed a higher bid, and he was off the hook for paying twenty dollars for a bucket of used car parts.

The rest of the afternoon passed quickly. Mibs had a delightful time, even bidding on several items. She stopped short of the winning bid for a set of handwoven baskets and dropped out when she felt the price went too high for a carved walnut music box. However, she was a happy auction bidder when she obtained an antique accordion-fold-out sewing box.

Tony bid on and purchased the items he had wanted. After pulling a few things out of a full crate of odds and ends, he packed them in his truck, then sold the remaining contents of the box to another buyer for just a few dollars.

By 4:00, both Tony and Mibs were hungry. They decided to forgo the restaurant trip and succumb to the enticing aroma of Italian brats sizzling on an outdoor grill in the food tent. They loaded their sandwiches with grilled onions and peppers, sat at a picnic table under the tent, and washed the food down with iced raspberry tea.

After the auction, Mibs thanked Tony for the enjoyable afternoon. She was delighted when he said he planned to take his auction purchases directly to his shop in Havendale. Then, he'd come over to Monahan's. Tony was insistent that he wanted to see the finished window display, but more importantly, to visit Aunt Bernie.

"Mirabelle," Tony said, "some of my fondest memories are the times I spent at your home. Aunt Bernie was there when I needed a mother figure after my mom passed away."

Mibs returned home, slightly sunburned but pleased with the afternoon's activity. She placed the wooden sewing box down for Aunt Bernie to inspect and then headed upstairs for a quick shower. By the time Tony reached the shop, Mibs had made some fresh lemonade.

"Anthony Vitali." Aunt Bernie scrutinized the young man as he entered from the back area where Mibs had let him in. "You've gotten almost as tall as your father."

"I consider a comparison to my father a compliment." Tony took Aunt Bernie's frail hand in his strong, smooth one. "It is wonderful to see you again, Aunt Bernie."

Chuckling, Aunt Bernie shook her head. "And just the same charm and charisma that Roberto had, too."

Mibs stood beside Tony. "We had a good time this afternoon, Aunt Bernie. I haven't had that much fun in quite a while."

Tony put his right arm around Mibs' shoulder. "Then we should definitely find other fun things to do. Now that I've found you again, I want to stay in touch." Smiling fondly, he gave her a one-armed hug. "Are you going to show me your display window?"

"Sure, come on." Mibs directed him to the front of the store, turning on a few lights along the way. After being amply complimented on her window design, she let Tony wander around the display and work areas.

"This is a nice place that you and your aunt have," he declared. "I had no idea this was such a classy fabric shop." With a gleam of appreciation in his eyes, Tony scanned the array of colorful material and sewing items. "Is business good?"

"We're getting more business than we can handle. In fact, Aunt Bernie and I decided to hire some help. Our first two employees start Monday."

"Fantastic! I'm glad things are going well."

Tony followed Mibs to the table where their drinks of lemonade waited.

"Sit down, Anthony." Aunt Bernie insisted that he visit for a while. After giving him a few minutes to quench his thirst, she placed her hand over his. "Tony, I wish things would've worked out differently with your father. He was a good man, and life was very unfair to him."

Tony's jaw muscles twitched, and his tone hinted at suppressed anger. "It wasn't life that was unfair." His tone rose in irritation. "It was his lying, deceitful boss and a lot of judgmental people who were unfair."

Aunt Bernie drew in a breath. "I'm so sorry, Tony. I didn't mean to upset you."

Rolling his shoulders, Tony made an effort to relax. "I'm not upset with you, Aunt Bernie. I could never be upset with you." He reached up and rubbed the back of his neck. "Dad has been gone three years now, and I thought I had made peace with the past. I call myself a Christian who believes in forgiveness, but I still fall short sometimes and let the anger wash over me."

Mibs spoke softly, "Tony, no one can fault you for being hurt. You can forgive, but I think it may take a long time for such a deep ache to fade."

Shrugging, the young man gently squeezed Mibs' hand, then reached for Aunt Bernie's open palm. "Thank you, Aunt Bernie. Thank you, Mirabelle. Two good friends like you are worth more than all the unfriendly people in the world."

~~

When she was young, Mibs wasn't fond of her name. She hadn't known any other girls with the name Mirabelle.

It was Tony who changed her mind. During the summer of Mibs' fourth grade, they were in summer Bible school again. That's when Tony found the meaning of *Mirabelle* on the internet. He said it came from a Latin word meaning 'wonderful.' He punched her in the arm – the odd way they showed friendship back then – and stated that when someone used her full name, Mirabelle, they were actually calling her *Wonderful.*

Ever since that day, Mibs felt content with her name.

Tony rose to his feet. "Well, I better get home. I still have some files that I should download and update tonight." He leaned over Aunt Bernie and gave her a long, gentle hug."

"I'll walk you out, Tony." Mibs looped her arm through his as they headed toward the back.

When they stepped out the door, Tony repeated, "I want to keep in touch. Call me sometime, okay?"

"I will. I don't want to lose track of you again, either. You're too good a friend." Mibs smiled and gazed into his warm, dark eyes.

Mibs stood near the open door and waved as he drove out of the parking lot. Thoughts of how Anthony Vitali had become a decent, hard-working man despite everything he had gone through kept her standing in the entranceway for several minutes. Finally stepping back in, she closed and locked the back entrance.

When she had all the shop lights turned off, she returned to the table and searched for her phone. "I guess I left my phone upstairs. May I use yours, Aunt Bernie?"

Aunt Bernie nodded and handed over her cell phone.

"Tony and I ate at the auction, but I'm getting hungry again. I forgot that I had planned to put some chicken in the crockpot this morning. Would you share a veggie pizza with me, Aunt Bernie?"

"I think pizza sounds good," her aunt agreed. "Maybe get them to add extra cheese?"

Mibs had just taken a big bite out of her second piece of the pizza, liberally covered with vegetables and warm, gooey cheese, when Aunt Bernie's phone rang.

Her aunt responded to the caller with a cheery voice, "Well, good evening, Jace." She gazed at Mibs. "Yes, she's right here. I believe she left her phone upstairs, so she wouldn't have heard when you called."

Not waiting, Mibs grabbed the plate with her pizza and her opened can of soda. She turned to hurry upstairs, stopped and pointed at the last of the pizza. Aunt Bernie nodded and mouthed, "Don't worry. I'll put the leftovers away."

Anxious to hear Jace's voice, Mibs hurried into her apartment, placed her food down on the coffee table, picked up the cell phone, and plopped down on the couch. Even though the phone rang within a few minutes, the wait seemed longer.

"Hi, Mibs." The familiar, rich baritone voice settled over her like a warm embrace.

"Hello, Jace. How are you?" Mibs exhaled a long breath and sank into the cushion.

They talked for over an hour, first exchanging words of endearment, then sharing stories about their busy lives.

Because of the nature of his job, Jace used a few cryptic words to talk about his work. He gave Mibs only a general idea of what he had been going through.

Mibs ended up laughing when she described how Tony unintentionally placed a bid at the auction. She vividly described the two ladies who would soon be employed at the shop, grateful that they would be starting in time to help with the costumes requested by the community theater. Mibs paused, listening carefully when Jace brought up the subject of William McBride.

"The sergeant that I'm working with made arrangements so I could talk to Willy's daughter, Catherine, while I was at a secure location. She told me her father was laid to rest in Arlington National Cemetery.

Apparently, several of his former military buddies were able to attend. I understand that the ceremony was patriotic and very emotional. I hope you don't mind, sweetheart. I told Catherine about you and your aunt. I explained that you were friends with Willy and his dog, Shadow, and that your thoughts were with her."

"Thank you for doing that, honey." Mibs' heart clenched at the thought of Willy's death.

"There's one more thing." Jace cleared his throat before continuing. "Catherine lives in a small apartment and works long hours. She can't keep Shadow and asked if I knew anyone who would give her a good home." Pausing briefly, he waited to see if Mibs would comment.

"Jace, I have a question."

"Okay. What's the question?"

"Maybe it's more of a statement than a question," Mibs reiterated. "I figure you have already told her that Shadow can come to Havendale." Mibs imagined the grin on her handsome detective's face as he replied.

"Yes, I did do that."

"Okay, so do Aunt Bernie and I get Shadow, or are you keeping her yourself?"

"How about we make it a combined effort? I'm at the office most weekdays, and sometimes my job keeps me out at night, too." Rustling papers could be heard over the phone. "I had them fill out a new form, which states that the owners of the Belgium Malinois named Shadow are Jace Trueblood and Mirabelle Monahan. I thought that when I'm at my house, even if I'm remodeling, Shadow could hang out with me. While I'm working, you and Aunt Bernie could enjoy her company. I guess it would be called shared custody."

"I would love to make Shadow a part of our family," Mibs blurted. "Since you talked to Aunt Bernie for a few minutes, did you mention Shadow to her?"

"Yes, Bernie liked the idea but said it would be up to you."

Mibs sighed. "Are you always so sure of yourself and expecting that I will agree to the plans you make? You already have the doggie adoption papers filled out." Mibs teased Jace, knowing that if she had hesitated, he would've stopped and listened to her wishes.

Jace chuckled. "Not expectin', just hopin'."

They talked for quite a bit longer, and neither wanted to end the conversation. Finally, Mibs and Jace both agreed that they had to say goodnight.

"You don't know how much I wish I were there with you." His long sigh spoke more than words.

"I miss you, too." Mibs gripped the phone tighter, praying that he would be home soon. "Goodnight, Jace."

"Goodnight, Mibs," Jace whispered.

Chapter 10

Jace hadn't been able to tell Mibs that he would be going out tonight. As soon as he hung up, he left the safe house and stealthily headed back to his hotel room. Forty minutes later, he was decked out in a charcoal-gray, satin-edged, notch lapel tuxedo and wore soft patent leather shoes. He dabbed on a bit of the expensive cologne, which had been found among the toiletries already in his hotel room when he arrived. He appreciated the subtle, spicy scent, and then noted the name on the bottle. *Not bad. I wonder if Mibs would like me to wear this once in a while.*

He was expected at a black-tie party given by a well-to-do businessman living in the area. Philip Clark was one of the people the task force had on their list, suspected of funding a chunk of the cost for the narcotics lab supplies. Jace was assigned the task of meeting and getting close to the businessman. This would definitely test his cover story as Nolan Lee. Fooling Clark would be more challenging than fooling members of the criminal group he'd already met.

A knock on the door interrupted Jace's thoughts. He picked up his Smith and Wesson M&P 9 and held it down at his side while he looked through the peephole. He unlocked the door with his left hand, swung it open and stepped aside, letting the man dressed like a hotel employee enter.

"Good evening, Mr. Lee. Here's the bottled Perrier you requested." The uniformed man walked over to the small kitchenette and placed three bottles of water in the minifridge. Then, turning back to "Mr. Lee," he said, "I understand that you have some dishes for me to take, too."

Jace slipped his gun into a holster, clipped to the back of his slacks. He let the tux jacket fall in place to hide the weapon. Nodding, he lifted the cover that had been on his lunch and placed a folded paper napkin on the plate. He put the lid back and handed the tray to the employee. "Thank you for taking care of this." The corner of Jace's mouth lifted briefly.

"No problem, Mr. Lee."

Jace closed the door after the man left, then sighed with relief. He was glad that the undercover policeman posing as part of the hotel staff had picked up the evidence that hopefully would identify William McBride's killer.

The cover story built for Nolan Lee must have been good, at least so far. Jace had been accepted by the local branch of the narcotics operation. He'd been allowed into the warehouse where the lab was located. He'd talked to several of their top-ranking members and been allowed to examine a sample of their product. While at the warehouse, Jace saw a man with a wound on his arm. The wound was undoubtedly an animal bite. He suspected that this could be the guy Shadow had bitten. Seeing the man discard a cigarette butt, Jace waited until no one was looking. Then, he used a napkin to pick it up and slide it into his pocket. That evidence was now on its way to the lab. The collected DNA would hopefully match what was taken from the scrap of cloth found in Shadow's teeth.

After checking his tie in the mirror, Jace took a moment to study the face looking back at him. He let the memorized persona permeate his mind. Tonight, he would allow himself to become the man behind the facade in the mirror—the personality of Nolan Lee.

Jace was surprised when he heard another knock at the door. This time when he peered through the peephole, he saw Matthew Brigham, assistant to Philip Clark.

"Brigham," Jace raised an eyebrow as he greeted the man. "I wasn't expecting to see you until later tonight."

Brigham held up a long, narrow package. "Mr. Clark asked me to bring you a couple gifts to welcome you to *the neighborhood.*"

Jace opened the door wider. Brigham stepped in, closely followed by a beautiful woman in a form-fitting evening gown. A second man, who walked a few feet behind Brigham and the woman, didn't appear to be the friendly type. His large size and height indicated that he would be a formidable foe to face. The odd shape of his nose suggested it had been broken more than once, and the straight, unsmiling mouth gave an ominous air.

Matthew Brigham saw him studying the big man. Pointing toward the guy, he said, "This is Mac. He's my enforcement support."

Smirking, Jace asked, "You mean your bodyguard?"

Brigham shrugged. He held out the package to Nolan. "Compliments of Mr. Clark."

Jace accepted the gift and pulled out the bottle of red wine. His eyebrows lifted in surprise. Fortunately, the background information that Jace had read covered the wealthy Nolan Lee's appreciation for fine wines. According to the cover story, Lee only drank costly red wines. A list of several of his supposed favorites – names, types, vineyards – had been included in the folder.

"A Cabernet Sauvignon from Screaming Eagle wines." He whistled low.

"Yes." Brigham nodded. "Mr. Clark heard that it was your favorite wine."

Jace nodded. "It is. It isn't easy to obtain." Placing the bottle of wine on a nearby coffee table, he asked, "And how did Philip Clark obtain this information? Sounds like he's done research on me."

Brigham dismissively raised his hands. "I think you expected him to." He studied Jace for a moment before adding, "Actually, we found very few people who've actually met you, Mr. Lee."

Jace put his hands on his hips and stared down at Brigham. "That's by design. I limit picture taking, and I only allow vetted people to get close to me. Is that a problem?"

"No, no," Brigham assured him. "We were able to find a few people who were willing to share minor tidbits about you, enough to know that you like fine wines, and..." The man turned toward the young woman who had been quietly standing a few feet away. "Fine women."

Oh, great! Jace thought. *Don't tell me that my other present is a high-priced 'escort.' Lord, please send an extra guardian angel to help me. How do I talk myself out of this without offending Clark?*

"Another gift?" Jace smiled as he made a show of running his eyes over the fair-skinned, doe-eyed brunette.

"Mr. Clark thought you might like some company." He gave the girl a wolfish grin. "Melody can accommodate anything you need."

"Is that right, Melody?" Jace moved closer and ran his hand down the bare shoulder of the girl he realized could not be much older than twenty. "Anything I need?"

For a fleeting moment Kent, a flash of fear crossed Melody's face. It was quickly replaced by a big smile. "That's right, Mr. Lee."

Letting his eyes linger on the girl for a moment, Jace wondered if she was an unwilling participant in tonight's activities. *Could he accept her company for this evening's party? Then somehow brush her off for the rest of the night. If this wasn't her idea of fun, maybe he could talk to Major Fleming about helping her. No. Too risky.*

"There *is* something I'd like you to do for me, Melody."

The anxious look in her eyes didn't fit her words or smile. "Yes, Mr. Lee? What would you like?"

"Be available the next time I visit the area." Nolan winked and squeezed her shoulder.

Sending up another silent prayer for guidance, he scrambled for a way to refuse the girl without offending Clark.

Turning back to Matthew Brigham, Nolan said, "Thank Mr. Clark for the excellent wine. And tell him I appreciate his generous offer of the *company,* but I prefer to find my own women."

Brigham was silent for a few seconds. He crossed his arms before responding, "That's fine, Mr. Lee. In fact, why don't you bring your own date to Mr. Clark's house tonight?"

"I'll see if she's available," Jace replied.

As soon as the two men and the woman left, Jace picked up the phone and dialed the number Fleming had given him.

"Bonnie's Place. This is Eduardo. How may I help you?"

Reminding himself that the phone was tapped and whatever he said would be heard, Jace chose his words carefully.

"Eduardo, this is Nolan Lee."

"Mr. Lee, what can I do for you this evening?"

~~

Major Martin Fleming had entered the control room a few minutes before the phone rang. When he heard the agent say the name Nolan Lee, Fleming stepped up next to the desk. He pushed the loudspeaker on the control panel.

"I have a last-minute request for my friend, Charlotte Evans."

Nolan had used the first name that came to mind. Charlotte Evans had been the name of the local librarian when Jace was young. Ms. Evans had spent a lot of time shushing him and his buddies when their voices rose in the library.

"I have a black-tie event that I'm attending tonight, and I've been encouraged to bring a companion," he explained. "I'll wait while you find her and bring her to the phone."

"Right away, Mr. Lee." The agent hit the mute button and turned to Fleming. "Who can we get on short notice?"

Turning to see who was in the room, Fleming spotted Jessica Moore. Jessica was fifty-three years old, short and plump, and had four grown children. She was also one of the best agents at doing voice characters. She could adjust her voice to sound like anything from a sickly old person to a young teen. Calling Jessica over, Fleming said, "Jessie, I need you to do your sexy voice. You'll be talking to a high-ranking member of a drug organization named Nolan Lee. You've been his 'friend' before, and he needs a high-class date for tonight." The major handed her the phone and stepped to the side.

As soon as Eduardo hit the mute-*off* button, Jessica was in character. "Nolan, sweety! You wanted to talk to me?"

"Hello, Charlotte," Nolan said in a warm baritone voice. "Baby, I know it's short notice, but I need you to put on an expensive evening gown and join me tonight. We have a party to attend."

"Oh, I love a good party!" She used a subtly seductive tone.

"It isn't going to be that kind of party tonight, baby. I need the company of a sophisticated lady."

"Of course, Nolan. You know that I can be elegant and refined if that's what you want. Will you be picking me up, or will I meet you somewhere?"

"I'd like you to be at my hotel room in an hour."

"An hour? You don't give a girl much time to get ready."

"I know, but I'm sure you can handle it, Charlotte. See you soon. And remember, it's formal dress."

Handing the phone back to Eduardo, Charlotte turned to Fleming. "Was that what you wanted, Martin?"

"Perfect, Jessie." Fleming sighed, then picked up a different phone and pushed an outside line as he mumbled, "Where can I find a fancy lady in a fancy dress in less than an hour?"

~~

Jace sat in front of the bar in his hotel room, tapping his finger on the counter. When a knock came a few minutes after eight, he peeked out to see who was on the other side of the door. Releasing a quiet sigh of relief, Jace pulled the door open and grinned at a stunning blonde in a black silk evening dress. The woman looked like she'd just stepped out of a fashion magazine.

"Thanks for coming over, Charlotte."

"Anything for you, Nolan." Trooper First Class, Tammy Karl, played her character well, giving him a coy smile.

Chapter 11

Nolan pulled the door of his hotel room shut and offered Charlotte his arm. They stepped into the elevator and pushed the button for the lobby. Just before the door closed, a blond, thirtyish man stepped in with them. Nolan had seen this man lingering around the hotel and suspected that he was one of Clark's henchmen.

The man exited the elevator with them. But instead of following them out the door, he pulled out a phone as he walked down a hallway.

Outside, a chauffeur opened the car door when Charlotte and Nolan approached the dark-gray Lincoln Corsair. As they drove away, Charlotte introduced the driver.

"This is Manuel Dias; he's with the DEA." Charlotte gave Manuel's cell number to him. "He'll help or notify backup if we call him."

"Mr. Lee," Dias said. "If you look in the cupholder in front of you, you'll find an item. I trust you know what to do with it."

He studied the chauffeur's cinnamon-colored eyes and tawny complexion before reaching for the small plastic container. He opened the two-inch square box and found a disk the size of a dime.

"It's both magnetic and adhesive, so it can adhere to most surfaces."

"I imagine it's pretty powerful and has good reception." Nolan slipped the small container into his pocket.

Dias nodded. "Considering its size, that listening device is very effective. If you place it in the desired room, it should pick up any voice within twenty feet."

A half-hour later, Nolan and Charlotte entered the Spanish-style mansion. A dark-suited man stood in the entranceway and greeted them. Nolan recognized the slight bulge in his jacket, realizing the man was armed. A second sentinel standing behind the first had massive arms that hung by his side like huge clubs, straining the seams of his extra-large suit jacket.

"May I have your name, sir?" the greeter asked.

"Nolan Lee. This is my guest, Charlotte Evans."

After a quick check on the iPad balanced in his hand, the man nodded at his beefy associate, who stepped aside, allowing Nolan and Charlotte to pass through the arched doorway.

A young woman in a well-fitting black-and-white uniform approached. She directed them down the hall and into a bright, spacious room. Two dozen-plus lavishly dressed people milled around the room, chatting and laughing. A string quartet played instruments on a small stage in the far corner of the room. Uniformed servers wove nimbly through the guests—some with trays ladened with flutes of champagne. Others held offerings of hors d'oeuvres and canapés.

Nolan plucked two glasses from the tray that appeared before them, handing one of the flutes to his companion. A slim, petite member of the catering team walked over with a silver tray. Charlotte selected a brie-filled, golden-brown puffed pastry. She popped the tiny treat into her mouth and smiled, reaching for a second before the girl moved away.

"Mr. Lee, I'm glad to see you found Mr. Clark's humble abode," Matthew Brigham said as he approached the couple.

"Brigham." Nolan nodded toward his date. "This is Charlotte Evans."

"Miss Evans." Brigham smiled broadly as he looked her over. "May I call you Charlotte?"

"Of course, Mr. Brigham."

"Oh, you must call me Matthew!" he insisted. "Especially since I'm going to keep you company later while Mr. Lee talks to our host, Mr. Clark."

Brigham offered Charlotte his arm. "Please, will you both come with me?"

As they approached their host, Nolan studied the average-looking man. Approximately five-nine, around 170, medium-brown hair. If he weren't wearing a custom-made tuxedo, Philip Clark wouldn't be someone who'd stand out in a crowd.

That impression changed when Clark turned, and Nolan saw his eyes. An image from the past flashed into his mind. He remembered strolling through a meadow on his uncle's farm years ago. He'd come across a badger standing over a mother rabbit and five babies. The vicious animal had killed all the rabbits, torn them apart. He had been within a few feet when he heard the badger hiss. He had looked down into malevolent, cruel eyes that manifested an inner meanness.

Clark's eyes had a similar glint of evil. Cold. Destructive.

Calling on the control he'd developed over the years, Nolan refused to let his repulsion show. He held out his hand and smiled.

"Mr. Clark, this is Nolan Lee," Brigham said.

"Good evening, Nolan. I've been looking forward to meeting you."

"Mr. Clark, thank you for inviting me to your home."

Over an hour later, the guests finished the full course meal prepared by Clark's in-house French chef.

The same uniformed woman who had greeted Nolan when he entered the home stepped up to the table, leaned over, and whispered, "Mr. Clark would like you to join him in his study. I'll show you the way."

As Nolan stood, Matthew Brigham approached with a bottle of wine and topped off Charlotte's half-full glass. "I'll keep Miss Evans company."

Nolan had a moment of disquietude about leaving Charlotte with the lecherous-eyed man. *She's trained. I'll do my job, and she'll do hers.*

Nolan entered the richly decorated study. Philip Clark stood by a sideboard and poured a dark amber liquid into a heavy crystal tumbler.

"Join me for a drink?" Clark asked. "It's twelve-year-old single malt."

Noland nodded. "Definitely."

As Clark lifted the decanter, Nolan leaned against the desk, slipping his hand under the edge and pressing the tiny disk against the wood.

It was after midnight when Nolan and Charlotte left the palatial house.

They climbed into the Lincoln, and after closing the door, Nolan turned to his companion. "I hope there were no problems after I left you with Brigham."

Charlotte shrugged. "He kept filling my wine glass. After a few minutes, I pretended to act a bit tipsy, giggling and smiling. That's when Brigham started asking me questions about you. He wanted to know if you talked about business or any of your associates."

"So. Brigham was trying to get information from you?"

"Yes. But I believe I convinced the creep that you never talked about business." Charlotte smirked. "I told him business was not what you had on your mind when you were with me."

Nolan chuckled. Then, he pressed her arm. "Thank you for showing up tonight and helping."

"Just doing my job."

Manuel glanced at Nolan in the rearview mirror. "Congratulations, Mr. Lee. You placed the listening device in a good location. I've been informed that the surveillance equipment is picking up a clear signal."

"Good! Now, let's hope Clark says something worth hearing."

~~

Three days later, Nolan Lee received a phone call.

"Hello, Mr. Lee, this is Eduardo from Bonnie's Place. I have your invoice ready to be picked up. I know you like to take care of accounting matters promptly."

Knowing that this message must be a code informing him that he should meet with Major Fleming or another member of the task force, Nolan responded appropriately.

"Thank you, Eduardo. You are efficient as usual. I'll stop by when I get a chance."

"Yes, sir. I'll see you soon."

He remembered that there were listening devices in his room and on the phone, so Nolan called the service desk to provide himself a cover for going out.

"Service desk. This is John. How may I help you?"

"Hello, John. I wonder if you could give me directions to the nearest branch of the First National Bank." Since he'd already researched the area, Nolan knew that the closest branch was only a few blocks away.

"Of course. One moment please." After a short pause, John was back on the line. "Sir, the nearest bank branch for First National is on this same street. Turn right when you leave the hotel and go three and a half blocks."

"Great," Nolan said, "I can walk from here. I could use a little fresh air."

Nolan took the short walk and entered the bank building. As he entered the revolving doors, he glanced back to see a blond man, who had apparently followed him from the hotel, stop and lean against the back of a nearby bus kiosk.

It appeared like the man would wait outside the bank until Nolan Lee came back out.

Good, Nolan thought. *You'll have a long wait.*

He made sure he was no longer in the man's sight, then he slipped out a side door and walked briskly to the back of the building. Twenty minutes later, he was in the designated secure building talking to Officer Mack Davidson, currently known as "Eduardo." With him were two other men and three women – all part of the ongoing task force. Nolan – now Jace – was only a bit surprised when Sergeant McCormick from the Broadly Police Department joined the group.

McCormick held out his hand, and the two men shook. "From what I've been told, the listening device you planted at Philip Clark's house has paid off."

"I was just getting filled in," Jace said. "Good to see you, although I was expecting Fleming."

McCormick smiled. "Fleming is rather busy at the moment. He's leading the team staking out a warehouse on the edge of the city."

"Eduardo informed me that they taped a conversation detailing a planned exchange between Clark's group and other heavy hitters in the narcotics chain."

McCormick nodded. "Fleming thought you deserved a chance to listen to the action. If it goes as planned, we'll be striking at the head of the snake. I heard that Philip Clark decided to attend this meeting himself. He would be a big catch."

"They're about ready," Eduardo suddenly announced. Everyone in the room became silent as he put the communication device on the loudspeaker.

The group stayed glued to the transmitter for the next several hours as they listened to the chatter between the various players handling the well-coordinated bust. They couldn't pick up everything said, but learned enough to know that their mission was successful. Many arrests were made, and a large number of illegal narcotics was confiscated.

Sergeant McCormick stepped away to answer a phone call. When he turned back, he had information for Jace.

"That was Major Fleming. He'd like you to come over for a debriefing at ten o'clock in the morning."

"Where?"

"Do you remember the federal building where you first worked out your cover story?"

"Yeah." Jace checked his watch. It was just past one in the morning. Weariness slipped through his voice. "Can I get a ride there?"

McCormick nodded. "Why don't you get a few hours of sleep first? There are some bunks in a room down the hall."

"Am I expected back at the hotel?"

"Nope," McCormick responded. "Sounds like our infamous Nolan Lee is gone. He took off and slipped out of the country." With a pat on Jace's shoulder, he asked, "How would you like to go home tomorrow, Detective Sergeant Trueblood?"

Chapter 12

The weather report for Monday morning promised a sunny and cloud-free day. When Mibs peered out the big display window at the front of Monahan's Sewing Shop, she saw the beautiful sky. She was also pleasantly surprised to see her new employee, Deanna Maxwell, standing by the entrance door. It was five before nine, and Mibs wondered how long the eager woman had been standing there. Mibs had asked her to be here by nine-thirty but told her that she'd be welcome to come earlier if she wished to learn the opening procedure. Mibs hadn't expected her to be waiting when she opened the shop. She dashed to the door, unlocking the latch and the security bolt.

"Deanna, good morning! Have you been waiting long?"

Deanna answered as she came inside, "Not at all. I parked in the back a few minutes ago and walked around to the front. I hope parking in the lot was the right thing to do."

"That was perfect. Thank you."

Mibs escorted her to a section in the back that would serve as a breakroom for the new employees. In the past, Mibs and her aunt had used a small couch in the shop's corner to take breaks. They had decided to devote a section in the back room near the office for their employees. With the help of a couple friends from church, they'd had the couch moved to the area, added a small table with chairs, and installed a refurbished set of lockers bought at a yard sale. Aunt Bernie had suggested that they even add a pair of café curtains to the single window in the corner to brighten the area.

"Would you like to put your things in one of the lockers? I have a couple unopened packages of padlocks if you want to use one, or feel free to bring your own." Mibs pointed out a basket holding the locks, note pads, pencils, and a couple of magazines. She guided Deanna to the kitchenette area. Mibs showed her where the hot water maker, the microwave, and the mini-fridge were. A door had been added to separate that area and the short hall, which led to Aunt Bernie's rooms. After Deanna had her purse stored away, they headed back to the front of the store and stopped at the counter. Mibs had prepared a checklist, which she used to go over the opening routine with the new morning employee.

She let Deanna sit next to Aunt Bernie and use the cash register, checking out customers that morning. Mibs and her aunt both believed that hands-on work was the best way to learn. When there were no customers in the shop, Mibs suggested Deanna use the schematic she had given her to understand where various items were situated on the floor.

By the time the first employee's shift was

almost over, the second new employee, Mary Wong, had arrived. Although Mary would work Tuesday through Saturday, she came in this afternoon for training. She, too, seemed to fit in well, impressing Mibs by her knowledge of different types of fabrics. Mary used a closing checklist that Mibs gave her that explained the end-of-the-day routine. When she left a few hours later, she graciously thanked Mibs and Bernie for the job.

By the time the shop was closed, Aunt Bernie and Mibs were more than glad that they had hired the two women.

Tuesday went by smoothly, with both Deanna Maxwell and Mary Wong eagerly learning the ins and outs of Monahan's Sewing Shop.

If the first couple days were any indication, Aunt Bernie agreed that within a few weeks, both employees should be comfortable watching the fabric store for a few hours by themselves if needed.

Since Wednesday seemed to be a slow customer day and Deanna was there to help Aunt Bernie, Mibs accepted a lunch invitation with a few of her friends. She planned on being gone for only an hour, so she met them at a local café.

"Hi, Mibs," Tegan greeted, tapping a chair. "Sit here, by me."

"We ordered appetizers," Olivia commented. "And since you need to get back to the sewing shop in a while, I also ordered iced tea for you.

I hope that was what you wanted."

"Perfect," Mibs responded. "Thank you."

By the time the waitress had taken Mibs' order for a chef salad, the appetizers had arrived. A large platter heaping with five different choices was placed in the middle of the table. Small, white ceramic dishes were placed in front of the ladies. The group shared the hors d'oeuvres while they waited for their various salads to be prepared.

The hour that Mibs had allotted herself passed by quickly. Seeing her Havendale friends and talking over old times and new times was a refreshing break she needed to do more often.

Tegan gazed at each girl. "Why don't we do this regularly? I certainly had a good time."

Sophie nodded. "Count me in."

Olivia offered to contact the others within the next few days to plan their next outing.

Signaling to the waitress, Mibs asked for her bill. The others did the same, pulling out their wallets.

"Oh, no!" Sophie exclaimed when she stuck her hand into the pocket of her jacket. She scanned the floor near her chair.

"What's wrong?" Olivia asked.

"When I pulled out the wallet from my jacket, I realized that I didn't feel the locket that I'd slipped into my pocket. The latch on the chain broke as I got out of the car, so I put it in my jacket. Now it's gone." Sophie frowned and sighed. "That locket belonged to my great-grandmother. My mother gave it to me last year."

All four ladies scooted out their chairs and searched for the missing piece of jewelry. Their efforts were unsuccessful, and Sophie seemed even more distressed.

"Wait a minute!" Mibs suddenly had an idea. "Let me see your jacket, Sophie."

Sophie slid the handkerchief-linen-material jacket off her lithe shoulders with a questioning expression and passed it to Mibs. Mibs slipped her hand into the garment for a moment before gazing up with a smile.

"I don't think you lost your locket," Mibs declared. "I think you just misplaced it."

Olivia, Sophie, and Tegan exchanged questioning glances. Then Sophie turned back to Mibs. "Misplaced it? Where?" she asked with a pleading tone in her voice.

Mibs turned the pocket lining of the jacket out and showed the others a three-quarter-inch hole in the material. "If you don't mind, I'm going to make this tear a little bigger."

Using small scissors, which she pulled out of a miniature sewing kit in her purse, Mibs made the opening just big enough to slide a hand through. Passing the jacket back to Sophie, she directed, "Now, slip your hand into the lining and see what you find.

With raised eyebrows, the surprised brunette did as directed. When Sophie removed her hand, she held the precious locket, as well as a penny and a dime.

Tegan started to laugh. "Mibs, you always did possess incredible powers of deduction. As I remember, you were often the first one to figure out a puzzle or problem."

"Well, I had an advantage in figuring this one out. When mending a pocket, I always check to see if there is a lining or space where an item could slip. It often happens in coats and jackets." Mibs gave a dismissive shrug.

"Thank you so much, Mibs!" Sophie said.

When Mibs returned to Monahan's Sewing Shop and drove into the back parking lot, she saw the delivery truck pull in behind her. This would be the first delivery made since William McBride's death. Mibs was sure that the new delivery person would be efficient, probably even a nice person, but it wouldn't be the same. She and Aunt Bernie already missed Willy.

Since Mary Wong had arrived for her afternoon shift, Mibs decided to show the new employee how to compare the order against the inventory sheet. Mibs checked with Aunt Bernie before leading Mary outside.

Mary, a quick learner, caught on to the simple task without trouble. By the time Mibs and her helper had accepted and checked off the delivery, stocked what they could in the sales area, and arranged the rest in the storage room, it was time to close the shop.

Aunt Bernie had taken care of the few customers that came during the interval. When the 'closed' sign was put up, the two Monahan ladies were ready to relax.

Chapter 13

When Thursday came around, Mibs felt confident leaving Deanna with Aunt Bernie. She headed over to Havendale Community Theater to take measurements for the six costumes commissioned by Mrs. Barns for the children's play.

Mibs pulled her Ford Taurus into the community theater's parking lot just before 10:00 a.m. Thursday morning. The sky was clear with a soft, warm breeze in the air. She hurried up the dozen wide cement steps, setting a basket down as she pulled open one side of the double doors. Using her foot to hold the door open, she picked up the basket and slipped into the building. The air-conditioning felt pleasantly cool as she entered the expansive auditorium filled with rows of stadium-style seats. As the seamstress made her way up the carpeted aisle, she heard children's chatter and laughter.

Mibs stopped to watch the young people constructing the set for the upcoming play, *The Unclassical Wizard of Oz*. The lengthy stage was divided into three sections, each representing a different scene from the play. The Gale farm in Kansas, where the cyclone struck, was open-ended with a clear view of the inside.

A second area divided into different parts depicted the Munchkin village, the

Scarecrow's cornfield, and the forest. Mibs could hear a volunteer directing an attentive group of teens painting on plywood-backed foam boards to represent houses, cornstalks, and trees. There was removable contact paper with a yellow-brick design that had been stuck to the floor in a wavy pattern.

Lots of green highlighted the Emerald City in the last section. Centered around the bright green backdrop were cardboard doors open to allow the view of the Wizard's chamber. A small part of the room, portioned off with a curtain, would be where the real Wizard hid. Mrs. Barns told Mibs that the stage crew would use a projector to supply the image of the Wizard's head. Apparently, this wasn't the first time this group had built a set. They were doing a praiseworthy job.

Heading to an open door on stage right, Mibs followed the voices up a set of steps. Mrs. Barns was there, along with a half-dozen adults and twice as many children. The coordinator glanced up as Mibs entered through the doorway.

"Miss Monahan," she chirped in her friendly voice. "Come in; come in!"

"Let me set these baskets down." Mibs cast her eyes around for an out-of-the-way spot. She didn't want anyone tripping over her sewing basket. Nor the smaller basket that contained various notions that she may need: threads, buttons, zippers, elastic, hem facing, and various other small sewing extras. Seeing an empty spot behind the partially closed curtain, she put the two baskets down and walked over to join Mrs. Barns and the group of young thespians.

Clapping her hands, Mrs. Barns addressed the group. "Attention, everyone. Attention. This is Miss Monahan, the theater's seamstress and costume maker." Making a 180-degree turn, the coordinator made sure everyone could see Mibs. "Please give her a rousing welcome."

A seemingly synchronized chorus of voices echoed around the enclosed area, "Good morning, Miss Monahan."

"Good morning, everyone." Mibs scanned the bright, eager faces. "Who's going to be Dorothy?"

A young girl with waist-length, brown hair and a stylish sweater and slacks outfit stepped up and spoke in precise words.

"Hi, I'm Geneviève. I'm playing Dorothy. My mom wants to help with my outfit, but sewing isn't one of her better talents."

"Hi, Geneviève." Mibs shook the girl's outstretched hand. "If your mother doesn't mind, the biggest thing she can do is to make sure you show up for the necessary fittings when your outfit is ready to try on."

"I'm sure that'd be okay with her," Geneviève replied.

"Okay, how about the Cowardly Lion?" Mibs questioned the gathered group.

A hand quickly shot up. "That's me!" a short

boy with fine, straight hair and slightly slanted eyes blurted out.

A special-needs student, the boy appeared enthusiastic about his part. One thing that made Mibs feel encouraged about working with the Havendale Community Theater was that they never turned down any young person who wanted to try out for a part in one of their children's plays. Mibs accepted his exuberant handshake. "I'm delighted to meet you. What's your name?"

"I'm Walter, but you can call me Wally. Everyone calls me that." His bright smile was irresistible. Mibs found herself easily smiling back.

A lady stepped forward and placed her hands on the boy's shoulders. "I'm Megan Meadow. I'm Wally's mother. Please, let me know if you need anything to help get the lion costume done."

"Thank you, Ms. Meadow," Mibs said. "I think we will have fun making the Cowardly Lion's costume."

The actors playing the parts of the Tin Man, the Scarecrow, and the Good Witch introduced themselves. Mibs, amazed at the casting job, could imagine the personalities would add spice to this children's play. The Tin Man was a tall, thin, eleven-year-old Asian-American boy. The Scarecrow's part would be played by a freckle-faced girl in fourth grade. An ebony-skinned young lady with rows of beaded braids had gotten the role of Glinda the Good Witch.

The only part that didn't seem to be covered was the Wicked Witch of the West.

"Does the play include the Wicked Witch?" Mibs turned to Mrs. Barns when no one stepped forward to claim that part.

"Well..." Anita Barns frowned. "We had a young lady scheduled to learn the lines for that part, but she came down with appendicitis. Shirley is doing fine, but her parents said she won't be able to keep the part." Gesturing to a portly gentleman with salt-and-pepper hair and wire-rimmed glasses, Mrs. Barns introduced Jeffrey Stewart. "Jeffrey is our children's coach. He helps them...learn their lines, listen for cues, find their mark on the stage, and learn the blocking...well, just about everything connected with the kids learning their parts."

With a bow, Jeffrey Stewart greeted Mibs. "We will let you know as soon as we've found a replacement for the part of the Wicked Witch of the West."

"That would be great. I certainly have enough to keep me busy for now." The remaining kids seemed to be younger than the children doing the main parts. "What about the rest of these energetic youngsters?"

"Ah!" Mr. Stewart nodded. "The remainder of our students will play the parts of Munchkins and monkeys." He turned to the other kids with a raised hand. "Our wonderful supporting actors! Right, group?"

"Yeah!" young voices rang out with a few

added, "Whoop, whoops."

"We splurged on the expense of ordering simple monkey costumes and matching Munchkin outfits for the youngsters," Mrs. Barns informed Mibs. "So, don't worry about sewing for them."

A sturdy-looking boy standing quietly behind the group of supporting actors stepped forward and cleared his throat. "Excuse me, Mr. Stewart."

Jeffrey Stewart turned when he heard his name called. "Yes? Mason, isn't it? What did you want to say?"

Mason took a moment to glance back at a stocky, muscular man with the same sandy-colored hair and gray eyes as him. The man gave the boy an encouraging nod. Clearing his throat again, he said, "Mr. Stewart, could a boy play the part of the Wicked Witch?" Taking another step forward, Mason stated, "I read that in the days when Shakespeare wrote his plays, the parts were performed by guys."

"That is correct. In fact, the parts were exclusively played by male actors," the coach confirmed. "Are you implying that you would like to try out for the part of the Wicked Witch, Mason?"

"Yes, sir." The boy hesitated for a moment, but then he stood up a little straighter. "Yes. I wanted to try out for a part, but I got back from baseball camp too late for the tryouts."

Jeffrey Stewart put his right hand on his chin and considered as he circled Mason.

"Hmm. Well, a good actor should be able to play any part, and since you will be in costume, I don't see why not."

A hopeful smile spread across the boy's face.

"However, you still need to read some lines. You have to prove that you can learn the part and play a believable character."

"Yes, sir." Mason pulled what appeared to be a rolled-up script from his back pocket. "Can I do that right now? When I got here, I heard that the witch's part was still open, so I've been reading it for the past hour."

Jeffrey focused on Mrs. Barns. "What do you think, Anita? Since I'm planning on working with the Munchkins and monkeys, I could let them listen to Mason's audition."

"Please, do!" Mrs. Barns answered. "It would be wonderful to have someone fill that part."

Turning to Mibs, Mrs. Barns gestured at the five main actors patiently waiting in front of them. "They're all yours, Miss Monahan." Clasping her hands and taking a deep breath, Mrs. Barns turned and headed to the central part of the stage.

"Who's first?" Mibs asked.

Everyone hesitated for a moment before the Tin Man held up his hand. "I'm Charlie Hyun. I'll go first." An elderly man standing near Charlie patted him on the shoulder, apparently a proud grandfather.

Mibs opened her notebook, neatly writing down each child's name, which character they would play, and the needed measurements. It didn't take long. Lena, the girl scheduled to play Glinda, would talk to Mrs. Barns about the headpiece and slippers to complete her costume. The ruby-red slippers for Geneviève would also be supplied by the theater group.

Three of the parents had stayed for the measurements and to see if they could be of assistance. Mr. Hyun and Ms. Meadow seemed especially intrigued with the material samples; silver lamé fabric for the Tin Man's outfit, and the Cowardly Lion's fake fur. After finishing the measurements, Mibs made arrangements to contact the children's parents when it was time for the first fitting. The others had just left to check with Mrs. Barns when Mason returned, happily announcing that he would play the part of the second witch.

"Wonderful," Mibs congratulated him. "I'm so glad you got the part and very impressed that you knew about the actors in Shakespeare's day. I'm especially pleased that you are willing to play the part. Unfortunately, many young men these days wouldn't have the grit to take on the challenge of playing the part of a witch. They'd be afraid that they would get teased."

"Yeah, well..." Mason rubbed his shoe back and forth across the floor, a slight frown tipping the edge of his mouth down. "I get teased about everything anyway, so I guess I'm used to it." Shrugging, he stood up a little straighter. "It doesn't matter, anyway."

Mibs could see a reaction to Mason's words on the face of the man standing a few steps behind him. It seemed apparent that it pained him to see the boy hurting. She pulled out the selected pattern, showing it to Mason.

"Your costume will be all black. I'll use lightweight cotton material to help keep you from getting too hot under the stage lights. You will have on green face paint and wear a wig. I believe Mrs. Barns will find the appropriate pointed witch's hat. Do you have black boots or black tennis shoes that you can wear?"

"Ah...black. I don't know." Turning around, he said, "Dad, I think I only have those brown boots and white tennis shoes."

His father stepped up. "No problem, son. We'll get whatever you need. Don't worry about it; I'll take care of it."

Mason gave his dad a grateful smile.

"Well, let's get your measurements and see what size pattern we will need." Mibs held out her cloth measuring tape.

"Ah, sorry. Will you have to buy a bigger pattern for me?" Mason asked humbly.

"Not at all. I only brought sample patterns for showing today. I don't order the actual patterns until I know the size and style needed."

He seemed relieved that he hadn't caused any extra work but mumbled, "I know I'm big for my age." Mibs wondered what unhappy experiences this boy had endured during his young life to have such a negative attitude about himself.

The same pained expression crossed his father's face. Stepping up next to the boy, the powerfully built man addressed his son. "Mason, there's nothing wrong with your size. You take after me, and I turned out okay." Leaning over the boy's shoulder, he asked, "Right? Didn't I?"

Mason rolled his eyes as he grinned. "Yeah, I guess you aren't too bad for an old guy."

Turning to Mibs, the man said, "Even though Mason just turned ten, he often gets mistaken for a twelve or thirteen-year-old."

Mibs regarded Mason. "When I was younger, I had the opposite problem. For a long time, I was the smallest kid in my class. I would get called 'pipsqueak' and 'squirt.' Those weren't the worst names used. It wasn't until I was in the last year of middle school that I seemed to sprout up like a weed. I'm 5'7" now and no longer feel like a...well, munchkin." Leaning forward, she whispered, "Just hang in there. It's hard sometimes, but keep believing in yourself. You'll be okay."

Mason scuffed his shoe on the floor again; this time, he smiled. "Thanks, Miss Monahan. You're nice." His focus wandered across the stage to where the other young actors worked, then toward his father. Mason said, "When I'm done here, I'm supposed to talk to Mr. Stewart to get caught up on what I missed. He said it would take about an hour."

"Okay, son. I'll just go get a cup of coffee and be back in a while to pick you up."

On her way off the stage, Mibs saw Mrs. Barns and mentioned that she had left her basket of sewing notions in the corner against the end of the curtain. There was no point in lugging it back and forth since she may need it again at the theater. There were plenty of spools of thread, snaps, and other sewing items at the shop.

As Mibs approached her car, she noticed Mason's father standing beside a well-used S-10 truck. He seemed to be searching for something on his phone. Pausing as she neared his vehicle, she decided to ask his name. "Hello." Mibs switched her sewing basket to her left arm and offered her right hand. "I don't think Mason mentioned his last name."

"Hi." He slipped his phone into his pocket and shook hands with Mibs. "My name is Michael Roberts, Miss Monahan."

"Please call me Mibs," she suggested.

"Call me Mike."

"Your son seems like a nice young man."

"He's a good kid." Pride mixed with a bit of worry echoed in his words. Giving his head a quick shake as if he were tossing off an unpleasant thought, Mike gave Mibs a questioning glance. "Would you know a place not too far away from here where I could get some coffee? We just moved to Havendale a few weeks ago, and I haven't gotten the lay of the land yet."

"Okay, Mike. I can show you my favorite place, the Blueberry Grove Café. They have great coffee, and I'd recommend their lunch if you're hungry." Mibs indicated the basket in her arm and pointed to her car. "Let me put this in the car; then, I'll give you directions."

Mike stepped up to her car and opened the back door. "Here."

"Thank you." After putting the sewing basket on the seat, Mibs pulled up the map on her phone and showed Mike where the café was. "It's several blocks away, but it only takes a few minutes to get there. I planned to grab something to drink myself. Maybe you would like to follow me there?"

With a shrug, the quiet but friendly man said, "Sure."

Ten minutes later, Mibs was pleasantly surprised to see several empty parking places on the main street near the café. Mike Roberts pulled into the spot behind her, and they reached the door to the little restaurant simultaneously. The pair entered and spied a few unoccupied tables.

"How about that one?" Mike pointed to the booth by the window. "That is, if you would care to sit with me."

"Sounds good to me." Mibs headed over and slid into the seat. Since it was almost noon, she decided to have a sandwich with her drink. "Are you hungry?"

"I'll wait to eat with Mason. If I know him, he'll be starving by the time I pick him up."

Mike scanned the menu. "But I'd like to see what they're serving here."

A short time later, Mike had his black coffee, and Mibs had her chicken salad on a croissant and iced tea. The café had a unique recipe for their chicken salad; they added celery pieces and pecans, something Mibs found tasty.

"You said that you just moved to Havendale. Do you have relatives here?" Mibs asked.

"No relatives. We came because of a job," Mike explained. "A buddy of mine knew I had just retired from the service. His brother-in-law owns a construction company in this county, and he'd advertised for a site supervisor. I've been working short-term construction jobs and wanted to find something full-time and permanent. It sounded like an excellent opportunity.

"So, you were in the military. What branch?" Mibs wondered.

"I served in the Navy Construction Battalion force of the U.S. military. Most people refer to us as Seabees."

"The Seabees." Mibs perked up. "My aunt's brother, Henry, served with the Seabees, but that was in WWII."

He nodded. "The Seabees have been around quite some time, definitely in the 1940s."

"Were you away from home a lot? I bet that was hard on Mason." Mibs bent down to take a bite of her sandwich, so a few seconds passed before she realized Mike had not answered; he'd gone silent.

<h1 align="center">Chapter 14</h1>

Mibs stared at Mike and wiped her mouth with a napkin. "I'm sorry. I said something that I shouldn't have. I never meant to ask an inappropriate question."

The former military man rubbed the back of his neck. "No. It's okay. You didn't say anything wrong. There's just a lot of baggage that goes with the fact that I was gone, that I wasn't with Mason for the majority of his life before he turned eight." Mike took hold of his coffee but didn't drink it. He sat, turning the cup in his hands. He glanced at Mibs, opened his mouth to speak but then shut it again. Finally, he said, "Miss Monahan...Mibs, Mason seems to like you, and maybe having a friend around would be a good thing for him."

She folded her hands and gave the man her full attention. Mibs judged him to be in his early fifties, weather-worn lines etched on his face, intelligent gray eyes that seemed to absorb what he saw. "I'll enjoy being Mason's friend and yours too, Mike."

Mike gave a slight nod. "You seemed to notice that my son doesn't have a lot of self-confidence, but I want you to know he is smart, real smart. I'm proud of my boy."

Mibs nodded but sensed his need for a quiet listener. "So, Mike, tell me more about you and Mason."

He hesitated before starting his story. "I had decided to make the Navy my career, my life. I didn't think I'd ever get married because I assumed that I would be deployed a lot, move around, and not be home often. This turned out to be true. But..." He paused, shaking his head, "I don't know if it was what people call a mid-life crisis or if I just got too lonely. I was forty years old when I met Shelia. She was pretty and fun, though half my age. We got married, and Mason was born within a year. Neither of us had planned on starting a family that quickly, but it happened." He shook his head. "Don't get me wrong. I've never regretted having Mason. He's everything to me." Unmistakable love shone from his eyes when he mentioned his son's name. "Anyway, I got deployed overseas shortly after the baby was born, gone for almost a year. When I got back, I could tell things had changed with Shelia. She was already tired of feeling like a single mom and wanted me to stay home more. I requested assignments stateside, and that seemed to help for a while. But when you're in the military, you go where you are needed. I ended up being sent out of the country again, this time for over six months. About four months after I'd been deployed, I received divorce papers from Shelia." Michael stopped talking and stared blankly for several seconds before he sighed and continued his story. "I was surprised. I guess I shouldn't have been. She had made it clear plenty of times that she wasn't happy. But I *was* surprised. I tried calling, but she never picked up. I left a message asking if we could try to work things out. She didn't call back. A couple weeks later, I received a note; all it said was, 'Mike, just sign the papers.' So I did. I never once failed to make sure the child support money was there on time. Mason was four by that time, and I saw him as often as possible in the next few years."

This time when he paused, he sat back and crossed his arms. "Mason had just turned seven when my battalion got back from helping in Puerto Rico and the Virgin Islands. The Seabees had been sent over to help clear and reopen major routes after the hurricanes had devastated the area. As soon as I was back stateside, I called Shelia's cell phone to see if I could have Mason for a few days. I wanted to spend time with him, maybe take him to a baseball game." Michael grabbed his cup and gulped down his coffee.

"Her reply was not only that I couldn't have him for a few days, but that she didn't want me to ever see him again. Not at all. She said she planned on marrying some guy she'd met, and he'd adopt Mason. I knew Shelia had dated off and on. That didn't bother me as long as Mason was cared for and happy. But I wasn't about to give up my son, especially to some guy I'd never met. I drove all night and reached Shelia's apartment by 8:00 the next morning. That's when I found out she'd moved out six weeks before and hadn't left a forwarding address. Right away, I called her cell phone, but I only got a recording saying the number was no longer in service."

If Mike had been holding a disposable cup, it would be crushed from the knuckle-whitening grip pressing on the sides of his ceramic mug.

Karen, the smiling, gray-haired waitress, stopped at their booth, holding a coffee pot in each hand. "Can I give ya a refill, mister?"

Michael nodded and slid his mug toward her.

"How 'bout you, Mibs? More tea?"

"No, thank you, Karen. I still have half a glass," Mibs responded.

As the waitress walked away, Michael Roberts rubbed the back of his neck again. "I'm sorry, Mibs. I'm basically a stranger to you; I don't know why I'm running my mouth. I doubt if you want to hear all this." Holding up his coffee, he blew on the steaming brew and cautiously took a sip.

Softly smiling, Mibs said, "You're talking, and I'm listening because I asked about your son and yourself. As soon as I met Mason, I liked him, so I wanted to know what makes him tick. And, since I'm a long-time resident of Havendale, and you're new in town, we should get to know each other." She picked up her sandwich and took another bite of the chicken salad. After following that with a couple sips of tea, Mibs said, "Besides, you can't stop the story now. You obviously found them since Mason is with you. What happened? How did you end up with your son?"

Raising an eyebrow, he asked, "Does everyone find it this easy to talk to you?"

Shaking the question off with a gentle shrug, Mibs said, "I like to listen. Sometimes people like to talk."

"Hmm." He paused, then resumed his account of how he found his son. "It took me almost a year to find them. I ended up going to the police since I supposedly had joint custody of Mason. They tracked Shelia down through DMV records, but they wouldn't tell me where she had taken my son. According to them, she showed them papers that listed her as having sole custody. Somehow, while I was overseas, she got a lawyer to put notices in some newspapers, papers she knew I'd never see. The notices had listed the time and place of a new custody hearing. Since I wasn't aware of the hearing, I didn't show up. Apparently, she'd even told the judge that she didn't have my address and couldn't contact me. She'd made it sound like I never had any contact with her about my son, never cared about Mason." He wiped his mouth with a napkin, his hands trembling.

"I resigned from the service and got myself the best lawyer I could afford. My lawyer used the same unfair tactics Shelia had used to set up a new custody hearing. She didn't show up at the appointed time. Plus, my lawyer had all kinds of paperwork showing that I'd always financially supported my son and had a clean, steady record. In the end, the sole custody ruling was reversed. I went back to the police department that had initially tracked her down, got the address, and drove five hours just to find she had moved again." Michael took a big breath, then let it out. "After 25 years in the Seabees, I'd made a few good friends. Let's just say with a bit of help, I obtained Shelia's new address and found out what kind of situation Mason was living in."

"The bum that said he would marry her and adopt Mason—some guy named Johansson—had dumped her within a few months of moving in with her. He and Shelia hadn't thought the sole custody thing through very carefully. She hadn't considered that leaving no forwarding address meant that child support payments would no longer reach her. As soon as Johansson had realized the cost of raising a kid was now on him, he bailed.

"It didn't take Shelia long to move on. By the time I found them, she was already living with some new guy, James Milton III." Mike chuckled. "How do you like that name? I got the impression that he's a lazy bum with a trust fund, living off family dollars for so long he wouldn't know how to hold down a job if he tried. Anyway, a couple of my buddies were with me when I showed up at his condo. We had to knock several times before the door opened. I was so surprised when Mason answered the door." For the first time since he began his story, Michael fully smiled. "Mason was surprised, too. His face lit up like it was Christmas morning, and he threw himself at me. I grabbed him, lifted him up, and pulled him close. We stood there, hugging each other. After a minute or so, we heard a slurred voice call out, asking who was at the door." Mike sighed.

"I marched in with Mason still clinging to my neck, Jack and Tim standing behind me." Mike sat back and folded his arms across his chest. A smirk settled on his lips. "I found Shelia and this Milton, both flying high as kites. Drug paraphernalia on the table in front of them. Shelia was so out of it that it took her a few moments to realize who had come in. By the time she focused enough to say something, Tim had pulled out his phone and started snapping pictures of the two of them and their *party favors.*

"I sat Mason down, told him to pack anything that he didn't want to leave behind, because he was coming with me. Shelia had managed to stand up by the time Mason came out of his room. The boy had a backpack over his shoulder, a laptop under his arm, and dragged a pillowcase holding the rest of his stuff behind him. I listened as my ex-wife sputtered something about how I couldn't take him, so I pulled out a copy of the new custody order and tossed it at her. Then I told her I planned to go back to court and get full custody. If she tried to fight it, I wouldn't just show the judge the pictures Tim had taken, but I'd also send copies to the police and all the local newspapers.

"She got angry, even tried to throw a punch at me, but ended up falling on her rear when she tripped over her own feet. That's when Milton 'the third' finally muttered something like – 'what pictures are they talking about?' I explained that we had taken photos of them using drugs with a minor in the apartment. That seemed to sink in. 'My father is an important man who wouldn't like that,' the drug-fogged idiot said. 'He doesn't like that kind of publicity.' I frowned at him and said that if he didn't want publicity, he should tell Shelia not to fight me for custody. The creep's eyes wandered around the room until he spotted my ex on the floor and said, 'Shelia, babe, don't fight the custody thing.'

"I just shook my head as Sheila started cussing, not sure if it was directed at Milton or me. My friends walked out with Mason and me, shutting the door behind us." With a wrinkled brow and melancholy tone, he added, "You know the saddest part? Mason didn't cry, didn't even tell his mom goodbye. He just glanced at her sitting on the floor, took my hand, and left with us."

Mibs sat there, trying to keep her mouth from hanging open. She was used to people opening up and talking to her. She had always had a welcoming personality that put people at ease. However, this was probably one of the saddest stories she'd ever heard. She leaned toward Mason's father. "Did your ex-wife try to fight you on getting full custody?"

"No. The lawyer sent her all the information—what, when, and where. She never showed up, and I haven't heard from her since." Michael tilted his head as he added the information he'd found out later. "My friend, Tim, had sent a copy of the pictures he had taken to James Milton's condominium. I believe that might have affected her actions."

Mike paused, then continued. "You know, the only other people I've talked to about this are my family and a couple friends."

"Thank you for sharing," she said.

"Thank you for listening." He stared at his empty cup.

"So, do you think the fact that you were gone a lot is the reason Mason is not as self-assured as he could be?"

"That was what I thought at first. I took most of the blame, but now..." Mike slowly shook his head. "There was a lot more going on while I was overseas than I realized at the time. Shelia kept him fed, clothed, and made sure he got to school; she didn't physically abuse him." A hint of anger permeated his following words. "She clearly didn't consider his mental health; just from what Mason has said, I worry that my ex-wife used him as a verbal punching bag."

Sitting forward and leaning his arms on the

table, Mike said, "After Mason came to live with me, I noticed that he apologized for every little thing. The other day, my son accidentally spilled a cup of water; I thought the boy would burst into tears, saying that he was sorry for being so clumsy. He put on a shirt last spring, and I commented about it getting a bit tight, thinking I should take him clothes shopping. He apologized for growing so much." Mike rolled his shoulders. "I don't know what his mother had been saying to him, but he has a lot of unreasonable guilt on his young shoulders."

The man sat quietly for a moment. "Anyway, I found a highly recommended pediatric therapist. Mason's been seeing him for almost a year now. My boy still has issues, but I think he's learning to deal with them."

"You found someone he can talk to, and you give him unconditional love." Mibs admired her new friend. "You're a good father."

"Isn't that what dads are for?"

"Hmm..." Mibs started to say more, but Karen interrupted, asking if they needed anything else.

"No, thank you, ma'am," Mike answered. "Please give me the bill." Checking his watch, he said, "Mason is supposed to be done in five minutes. I'd better get back over to the theater."

"Go ahead and take off," Mibs instructed him. "I'll get the bill. Maybe we can have coffee again sometime?"

Rereading his watch, he nodded, "Okay. I'll owe you a coffee sometime."

"Don't worry, Mike. They aren't going to let your son leave until you get there. I've gotten to know a lot of the local theater group; they're good people."

He smiled and gave a short wave as he hurried out of the restaurant.

Chapter 15

When Mibs returned to Monahan's Sewing Shop, she asked Aunt Bernie how things had gone while she was at the theater. Her aunt informed her that business had been steady but not too busy, giving Deanna time for other jobs between customers. Mibs found that the new employee had worked through several bins of back stock, filling empty hooks on the pegboards and straightening the material section.

Mibs pulled out the notes for the children's costumes and began marking down order numbers for patterns to figure out the kinds and amounts of fabrics and notions needed. By the time she had placed the orders, Mary Wong had come in and signed in on the computer to start the afternoon shift.

The short overlap of time between when Mary's shift started and Deanna's ended gave them a chance to talk about what had been done that day and what still needed to be accomplished. Mibs walked to the pattern rack with Mary, giving her the inventory form for the Butterick, McCalls, and Simplicity patterns. They needed to determine which ones had been sold and needed to be replaced; hopefully, their tally would match the inventory listed on the computer.

Mibs and Mary concentrated on the open drawers containing the various patterns, ignoring the next person who entered the shop.

~~

Mibs and Mary didn't see Bernice smile and move to the small kitchen area behind the counter, where she opened a Mason jar and pulled out dog treats.

Well-behaved as always, Shadow padded in with Jace. She wagged her tail eagerly as her eyes followed the biscuits that Bernice held out to her. Jace followed behind the dog, leaned down, and set a food bowl near the minifridge. He took a moment to fill a water bowl from the small sink and place it down, too, then searched out a spot to toss the royal blue dog bed he had tucked under his arm.

"Would this be okay over here?" He asked and waited for Bernice to nod before placing the soft bed in an out-of-the-way corner. Leaning down and giving the old woman a hug, Jace said, "How are you, Bernie?"

"Better now that you're back," she replied. As she watched Jace turn and survey the sewing shop, Bernice pointed toward the back area. "She's working by the pattern files."

~~

"Thanks, Bernie." With quick steps, it didn't take long for him to cross over to the far side of the shop and move around a rack of quilting bundles. Jace couldn't help releasing a deep breath upon seeing Mibs by an open drawer, both hands full of pattern envelopes.

Mibs must have sensed a presence behind

her. She froze in place for a moment before slowly turning around. Mibs' mouth stretched to a wide smile.

"Hi, Mibs." Jace opened his arms in a welcoming gesture.

"Oh!" Mibs' voice bubbled with excitement. "Oh," she said again before practically throwing the patterns she held into Mary's hands and happily moving into Jace's arms.

Jace hugged his girl after having been gone for too long. He wanted to kiss her. But noticing the two employees, three customers, and, of course, Aunt Bernie, he hesitated, considering the propriety of such a public display of affection. Mibs gazed into his eyes and smiled. That smile, as always, took his breath away.

Mibs murmured, "I missed you."

Jace turned and looked down when he felt a push against his legs.

"Shadow!" Mibs knelt and rubbed the black-masked, mahogany-colored dog. "How are you doing, pretty girl?"

While Mibs welcomed Shadow, the petite, dark-haired employee had politely turned away. "Hi. How are you?" Jace asked.

Mary peeked up shyly. "Um, I'm fine."

Half standing while still petting Shadow's head with one hand, Mibs said, "Mary, this is Jace Trueblood. Jace, this is Mary Wong, one of my two new employees."

After Jace and Mary exchanged greetings, Mibs directed Jace to the new employees' break corner and introduced him to Deanna as she gathered her things to leave for the day. As soon as they were alone, Jace pulled Mibs into his arms.

"Are you home? Do you have to go back?" she eagerly asked.

He touched his head against hers, "I'm home. We pulled in members from the drug network covering the surrounding four states. There are others still working in the task force to follow it further, but I'm done. I'm home."

"What about..." Mibs leaned back and scanned his face. "What about Willy's killer?"

"Two men are being charged with his death: Newman and Pullman. Shadow had bitten one of the men who attacked Willy, and the lab was able to match a DNA sample to a suspect, Newman. As soon as we showed him the DNA proof, he started spilling his guts. And...when we arrested Pullman, he had a gun on him that matched bullets that had shot Willy." With an air of satisfaction, he added, "They're both going away."

"I'm glad they can't hurt anyone else now." An expression of pain clouded her eyes for a moment. Taking a quick breath, she asked, "Did you have any major problems while you were working undercover?"

Jace hesitated, running his hand through his hair. He thought about Trooper Tammy Karl, who had taken on the character of Charlotte Evans, and about the tension he'd felt while placing a listening device in Philip Clark's den.

Since McCormick and Fleming had a warrant for the listening equipment, they had been able to record incriminating conversations between Philip Clark and others. When an exchange of money for narcotics had been scheduled, members of the task force were there and had pulled in a number of the culprits.

"Well...I can't talk about it yet. The task force wants the team to keep quiet about certain things while they track down remaining leads. As soon as they complete the investigation, and if they give the okay, I'll tell you everything I can about the case. I can say that I met some interesting people and had to do some creative improvising a few times. But for the most part, the assignment went as planned, and we were able to shut down a big part of that particular cocaine syndicate."

Jace caressed the side of her face. "Sweetheart, do you think you can leave early, maybe in a couple hours? I want to head home, check my mail, and take care of a few things. I can return around 4:00 and take you out for an early dinner; we could spend a quiet evening together."

Mibs' face flushed with happiness. "Yes, especially with Mary here to help Aunt Bernie close up the shop. I could be ready whenever you get back."

Giving her a quick kiss and reluctantly stepping away, Jace promised to be back later. Walking to the front, he stopped to clip the leash onto Shadow's collar. "Let's go, girl. I want you to see your second home."

~~

Mibs walked Jace and Shadow to the door before turning back around. Aunt Bernie and two white-haired ladies were standing by the counter, all three with smiles on their faces.

"You're happy to have Jace back," Aunt Bernie said.

"You know I am," Mibs replied and greeted her aunt's two friends. "Hello, Hazel. Hello, Marge."

"You have a very handsome beau." Hazel spied over half-glasses at the girl; Marge nodded in agreement.

Mibs bit her lower lip in an attempt to tame the wide grin that spread across her face. "Thank you. I think so, too." Moving away from the trio of octogenarians, she headed toward the back area of the store. "I better help Mary finish inventorying the patterns. I want to have time to go upstairs and change before Jace gets back."

~~

When he reached Maple Street, Jace walked Shadow around his property's perimeter to let her get some exercise and give the dog a sense of the boundaries. After being gone for over a month, the detective wasn't sure if a floor full of envelopes would greet him. The mail slot in the front door of the hundred-year-old Georgian Colonial was convenient, but he hadn't thought to set a box below the opening to catch the items that the postal workers slid through. He cautiously pushed the door open and was surprised not to find the expected scattered mail. A large fruit bowl, which he recognized as having come from the kitchen, had been placed against the wall just past the entrance. He surmised that Brice Long had taken the time to collect the mail and place it in the container.

Jace was glad he'd left a key with Long. When Long had found out that Jace would be gone for a while, he'd told Jace that he'd check on the house while the detective was out of town.

Jace gave Shadow a quick walk-through of the first floor, then started up to his refinished master suite. After the first couple of steps, he realized that the dog seemed to be having trouble going up the stairs. "Hey, Shadow, I'm sorry. You're not completely recovered from the surgery, are you?"

When the police had brought the wounded dog into the veterinarian's office with a bullet lodged in her body five weeks ago, the vet hadn't been sure the Belgium Malinois would survive. Thankfully, she'd pulled through but seemed to be having trouble getting her full strength back. This had been the second time the military-trained canine had struggled to survive from serious wounds; the first time was from a firefight in Afghanistan.

Jace stooped down and picked up Shadow, carrying the dog to the top of the steps.

Placing her on the parquet floor of his bedroom, he directed the dog to stay as he hurried back to the truck for things he had bought for the dog, two of each: dog beds, bowls for food, and bowls for water. Along with the other items, Jace had also gotten the recommended brand of dog food.

William McBride's daughter, Catherine, had given Jace only a little information on caring for Shadow. One of the things that she had said was rather than giving the dog a treat for good behavior, Willy had kept a small orange ball on hand. Showing the ball to Shadow meant that she earned extra playtime. The more times she saw the ball during the day, the longer her playtime would be that night. Jace wished he'd picked up a ball and a few dog toys.

He went through the mail, showered, and changed, then he called the Havendale Police Station to let his men know he'd be there early the following day. Jace took more time than he'd planned. Realizing that it was almost 4:00 p.m., Jace carried Shadow back down the stairs and hurried out to his truck to drive the five minutes to Monahan's.

When he pulled up in front of the sewing shop, Jace noticed a group of women entering the store. Following them in, he could see that Mary Wong and Aunt Bernie were extra busy. Mibs was coming down the stairs from her apartment, catching sight of the extra customers. Jace noted the question in Mibs' eyes as she searched his face for understanding.

He winked at her. "Go on. I know you need to help." He stepped into the kitchenette with Shadow to get out of the way. He opened a teddy-bear-shaped cookie jar and swiped a few coconut macaroons. Shadow curled up by his feet as he waited. It was almost 5:00 p.m. when the last customer left. A few minutes later, the shop was closed, and Mary headed out the door.

Even though they were leaving an hour later than planned, Jace and Mibs tried to persuade Aunt Bernie to join them. She graciously declined the invitation but did accept the offer to have something from the restaurant brought home for her. When they returned after dinner, Shadow, resting her chin on the old aunt's lap, seemed content to stay downstairs. Jace and Mibs settled on the sofa upstairs and watched one of Mibs' favorite movies, *The Princess Bride*. Jace felt happier at that moment, with his right arm around his girl's shoulder and his left hand secure in hers, than he had in weeks.

Chapter 16

Friday morning brought an unexpected but welcomed flurry of customers. It was late morning before Mibs could start on the first costume for the play. She would have to wait for the patterns and fabric for a couple of the outfits but had the needed supplies for Dorothy, the Scarecrow, and the two witches. Mibs cut around the pattern pieces for Dorothy's jumper, and then the seamstress placed them on the blue-and-white gingham material. Once she made sure that the pattern pieces were lying precisely on the straight grain and the bodice piece pinned along the fabric's fold, she began cutting.

Mibs had assigned the two new employees each a costume to make. Having worked with fake fur before helping with the school plays, Mibs knew Deanna would feel confident tackling the Cowardly Lion's suit. Mary would sew the Tin Man's outfit. After discussing the pattern and needed material, they decided to use silver lamé with heavy interfacing between the outer fabric and the lining. The stiff interfacing would give a more substantial, 'tin' appearance to the costume. While waiting for the material and supplies for the other projects, she had Deanna and Mary turn the plaid shirt and overalls into the Scarecrow's clothing. In between, of course, the employees were taking care of customers and any needed sewing repairs or alterations showing up at the shop.

By the end of the following week, Mibs had called Geneviève–aka Dorothy–Angie, the freckled-faced Scarecrow, and the Wicked Witch of the West, Mason. Their costumes weren't done, but they were ready for a first fitting. Dorothy's jumper and blouse would need minor adjustments. The Scarecrow's costume should only require the added hat and makeup.

Mason came in to try on the Wicked Witch outfit just before 5:00 p.m. Even though he wanted a part in the play, Mibs could tell that the ten-year-old boy became embarrassed when he stepped out wearing the black dress. "I kinda wish the witch wore black slacks instead of a skirt."

"It wouldn't have the same effect." Mibs shook her head. "Besides, this part will better show your acting abilities." Leaning toward him until he looked at her, she said, "That's the main reason to play this part. Right, Mason?"

Scuffing his shoe along the floor, he shrugged. "Yeah, I guess so."

"If you show them what a great actor you are in this part, they are very likely to let you play characters in future plays."

"Yeah, maybe." Mason gave a crooked smile.

"Hmm, I got the sleeve a little long and the hem a little short; nothing I can't fix." Mibs pulled a few pins out and started making adjustments.

While Mason tried on his costume, his father, Mike, waited near the front of the store, having a lively conversation with Aunt Bernie and giving Shadow some appreciated attention. Most of the customers seemed to enjoy the dog's presence whenever Shadow trotted in from the back area. However, there were a few people who had been leery of the medium-sized canine.

Mibs had added a gate between the end of the counter and the wall. This seemed to appease any less-than-enthusiastic customers about the dog. Even though Shadow could quickly push the magnetic latch on the gate to open it, she would not do so unless given the appropriate signal.

By the time Mibs walked to the front of the store with Mason, Mary Wong had left for the day, and Aunt Bernie had turned the sign to *Closed.* Michael and Mason left, and Mibs locked the door.

"We've been doing a good job of eating healthy lately." Mibs scrunched her face as she addressed her aunt. "What would you say if we splurged and had some junk food?"

"Hmm." Aunt Bernie raised her eyebrow. "How about cheeseburgers and shakes?"

"Oh, yeah. Benji's Grill!" Mibs pulled out her phone. "I'll call Jace and see if he'll be done working soon; maybe he can meet us there."

Twenty minutes later, a fully-loaded

cheeseburger was placed on the table in front of Mibs. "Mmm," she hummed just as the restaurant door opened, and Jace walked in.

His soft-brown, single-breasted suit and burgundy tie was more formal than the jeans and t-shirts most patrons wore in the burger and brats eatery. Mibs remembered that this was the outfit that Detective Sergeant Trueblood had been wearing the first time she saw him on the porch of the Hornsby's brick and stone house. It had been the first time she had glimpsed those expressive blue eyes.

"Hi, honey." Mibs gave him a bright smile.

Pulling out an empty chair, Jace sat down. "Hi, Mibs. Hi, Bernie. How are my girls doing this afternoon?"

"We're doing well." Aunt Bernie's head tilted as she stared at Jace. "You, however, seem a little tired."

Mibs decided not to point out that she, too, noticed the apparent fatigue. Instead, she asked, "Are you hungry, Jace? Would you like something to eat?"

He released a deep breath. "I'm going to get a sandwich to go. I've been playing catch up with things that piled up while I was gone. Now, we have a hit and run that we're working on."

The waiter sat a frosty glass of chocolate malt in front of Mibs and a strawberry shake next to Aunt Bernie. "Would you like to order, sir?" he asked Jace.

"Yes, I'd appreciate it if y'all would fix me a

cheeseburger with everything. Please make it to go.”

“Would you like a drink to take with you?”

“No, thanks.”

Mibs reached over and placed her hand on top of Jace’s. “You have to go back to the station?”

“Yeah. After that, I’m headin’ over to the hospital. The hit-and-run victim was a twelve-year-old girl on a bike. She just came out of surgery, and I want to get over there and talk to her parents.”

“Oh! That poor child,” Mibs said.

“Do the doctors think she’ll be okay?” Bernie asked.

Jace nodded. “She survived the accident but will need time to recover, probably physical therapy, too.”

The waiter returned, placing a brown bag with the Benji’s Grill logo on the table. Jace started to pull out his wallet, but Mibs stopped him and turned to the waiter, telling the young man to put Jace’s sandwich on her bill. The weary detective sat back and sighed.

“Would you two mind if Shadow spent the night with you? I don’t know how late I’ll be working, but I’m sure I’ll head back early tomorrow.”

“Of course, she can stay,” the two ladies answered.

Jace stood up and grabbed the bag of food, and then he gave Aunt Bernie a gentle squeeze on her shoulder before leaning over and kissing Mibs on the cheek. "I'll try calling tomorrow."

Mibs, disappointed, watched her law-enforcement boyfriend leave, before slumping back in her chair.

"He'll be all right," her aunt assured her.

"I know. It's just hard sometimes." Mibs sat forward and reached for her shake. "I understand that caring about him means accepting his job and everything that comes with it."

Chapter 17

Deanna and Bernie had things running smoothly at Monahan's on Tuesday morning when Mibs left with her car's back seat full of costumes. She made her way over to the Havendale Community Theater and carried the first box of outfits inside. Before the seamstress was halfway down the aisle, several young people, including Angie and Mason, came hurrying over to assist. With the extra hands, everything was brought into the building in only two trips.

The morning moved along quickly, as the young actors were cooperative and the parents on site were helpful. Munchkins and monkeys meandered around the stage as they were shown the location of their specific spots. Geneviève agreed that her Dorothy costume fit perfectly, and Angie would work with Mrs. Barns to get the finishing items for the Scarecrow. The black tennis shoes Mason's dad had bought him blended with the skirt's black material, which had been lengthened to fit the boy's height. The silver lamé had arrived for Charlie Hyun's Tin Man costume, and it hadn't taken Mary long to construct the outfit. Charlie was joking with Mason; they were trying to decide who had the more outlandish costume. Mason insisted that when he had on the green face paint, he would be one scary witch. Charlie concluded that the material's sparkle and his silver makeup would make his costume more noticeable on the stage.

Mibs waited outside the two dressing rooms as Mrs. Meadow helped Wally don his Cowardly Lion outfit for a first fitting. The boy's voice could be heard through the door. Wally didn't seem happy about something. The door opened partway, and Mrs. Meadow poked her head out.

"Miss Monahan," Wally's mother called in frustration, "Wally has a question for you."

Mibs stepped forward as the special-needs student shuffled out of the dressing room.

Glancing up shyly, he asked, "Can my costume be two parts? It feels funny being all stuck together, and it's hard to get on."

Mibs considered the one-piece outfit; the wearer had to put his legs into the lower section, pull up the top, slip his arms in, and then have the long zipper in the back closed. Deanna had done an excellent job on the costume. Although it would be more work, she assured the boy, "If that's what you'd like, Wally, then I'll make it into two pieces." Mibs leaned down so she could see his face, his lower lip beginning to quiver. "Hey! It's no problem."

"You sure, Miss Monahan?"

She moved her hand in a dismissive gesture. "It's a piece of cake, Wally." She tapped herself on the shoulder to lessen the boy's discomfort. "Especially for a seamstress extraordinaire."

"Thank you, Miss Monahan." Wally grinned.

A moment later, Lena–the Good Witch Glinda–stepped out of the other dressing room. Her costume was more elaborate than the others. The full-length, full-skirted gown featured layers of organza and tulle in soft blue hues. Mibs had only basted the dress's seams because she wanted to make sure the Cinderella-style costume fit before sewing the finished seams in the delicate fabrics.

With her pin cushion around her wrist, Mibs knelt to make several needed adjustments to the beautiful costume.

Lena's smile dazzled as she modeled the gown. "It's so pretty!" the young girl bubbled.

"You make it even prettier," Mibs told the petite African-American actress. "Okay. I have what I need marked. Be careful when you take it off so the pins don't stick you."

Lena's grandmother, who had accompanied her today, nodded. "I'll help her change."

After removing the costume, the girl hurried over to join the rest of the team as they practiced on stage. Wally waited calmly with his costume slung over his arm. His mom stood nearby.

Mibs turned her attention to Wally. "Let me take a few extra measurements before you head over and listen to Mr. Stewart and Mrs. Barns."

"Okay." Wally handed Mibs the costume and held his arms out, standing perfectly still to allow her to use the measuring tape again.

She had finished writing down the number

of inches needed for the adjustments and glanced up in time to see a man slink behind the heavy maroon curtain gathered at the end of the stage. The dark-clothed man ducked his head and moved quickly out of sight.

Mibs wondered how he'd gotten through the back door, which was usually kept locked. Wary of a stranger in the building, Mibs decided to seek out Mrs. Barns and ask if the unknown guy had a reason to be sneaking around the theater.

Turning back to Wally and his mom, Mibs said, "You can head on over and join the other performers if you like, Wally. Mrs. Meadow, I'll call you as soon as I have the outfit ready to try on."

"Thank you." Mrs. Meadow squeezed Mibs' hand. "Thank you so much."

Mibs folded the lion suit and placed it in a tub. She wanted to check the basket full of notions to see if it contained a few shorter zippers to replace the longer one on the back of the one-piece lion outfit. However, she decided to first ask the theater director about the questionable man she'd seen.

Mibs moved through the open door, gazing at the gathering of people in the middle of the stage. The children's acting coach, Jeffery Stewart, had asked any available parents or guardians to come to the first few practices. Stewart wanted the moms and dads to help the young actors learn their parts. The best way they could do that would be to understand what was required of their child. Mibs walked forward, then saw several people she knew, including Mason's dad and a few men and women from her church.

She had taken only a half-dozen steps when two loud bangs like a car backfiring echoed through the auditorium. Things went silent for a few beats as everyone wondered what caused the noise.

Suddenly, one of the smaller munchkins screamed, "Daddy!" The dark-haired, brown-eyed child ran forward, sinking to her knees. Her father was on the floor, and screams bellowed from the girl's mouth, blood pooling around the man's body. Another man leaned forward–Mike Roberts?–clutching his shoulder.

Call 911, Mibs silently commanded herself. She reached into her pocket for her phone before remembering that she had left it sitting in the tub of costumes. Turning and running back through the door toward the costume container, Mibs crashed into a solid body. The collision knocked her to the floor. She heard a curse, then Mibs focused on the voice and got a second view of the dark-clothed man who had snuck by a short time before. Angry, vicious eyes stared down at her. A black, hooded sweatshirt didn't completely hide the dirty blond hair and narrow chin. After knocking her down, the armed stranger hesitated a moment before aiming. Mibs quickly rolled over, moving onto her knees in preparation for a dash away from the gunman, hoping she could avoid being shot. But, before he could pull the trigger, several women's loud, scared voices surged through the door, causing the man to turn and run toward the exit. Mibs sank back down, now shaking from shock. She pulled herself together, found her phone, and finally called 911. Two moms, each clutching a child, ran to seek refuge in the bathrooms.

Still trembling, Mibs forced herself back onto the stage to see if she could do anything to help. The whole crew seemed shaken; several people were standing around and crying. Others had also called for an ambulance and the police. Several parents and children were still crouching behind scenery, boxes, anything that would offer cover, afraid to come out. One of the parents had picked up the now-hysterical little girl whose father lay motionless on the hardwood floor, holding her close and trying to comfort her. Someone pressed a cloth on the man's chest, but it became apparent that it was a futile gesture.

Mike Roberts sat on the floor with most of his back against the wall. Jeffrey Stewart held folded towels to Michael's shoulder, putting pressure on the bullet wound, one pressed against the back, and one the front. The entrance and exit wounds indicated that the bullet had gone completely through. Mason knelt on the other side, trying to be brave and forcing back tears. He held his father's hand.

Mibs made her way to Mason and his dad. "Mike, how can I help?"

With bleary eyes, Mike blinked and focused on Mibs. "Mibs, can you take care of Mason for a bit? I think I'll have to go to the hospital and get my shoulder patched up."

"Of course, I will."

"No!" Mason retorted. "Dad, I'm not going to leave your side!"

"Mason." Mibs put her arm around Mason's shoulder. "Listen to me."

The boy reluctantly turned away from his father. "I have to stay with him."

"I understand." She nodded. "But when the EMS gets here, your dad will need to be taken to the hospital. Come with me. We'll follow them, and I'll wait with you while the doctors treat him."

Mike patted his son's hand. "You go with Miss Monahan, Mason. Do what she says. I'll probably just need to get a few stitches before we head home."

"Okay, Dad." Mason nodded through glassy eyes.

Chapter 18

The ambulance arrived quickly, and an EMT worked on Mike Roberts' shoulder, applying temporary bandaging. After checking Jacob Beam, the fatal gunshot victim, the second EMT turned to his partner and shook his head. He moved over to help with Roberts, then he pulled out an IV and inserted it in the back of Mike's left hand.

The first police officer on the scene had directed everyone else to move to the auditorium's seating area. Filling the middle front two rows, the stunned group murmured in stunned confusion as they waited for further directions.

Mibs sat with her arm around Mason at the end of the first row. The boy's eyes never left his father as the paramedics worked on his dad.

~~

Less than ten minutes after the uniformed police and the ambulance crew had arrived, Detectives Jace Trueblood, Juan Mendoza, and Gene Delgado tromped down the outer aisle.

Jace glanced over at the assembled people in the seats facing the stage. He slowed his step for half a second when he realized that Mibs Monahan was among the waiting witnesses, before he hurried up the steps and across the stage.

"You two know what to do," Jace said over his shoulder to his two top detectives. "Let me know if you find any spent shells. Make sure the hospital knows to keep the bullet slug that hit the victim they're loading on the stretcher."

One of the emergency technicians heard Trueblood's order and turned toward the three detectives. "They won't find a bullet when they work on him. It was through and through." The EMT pointed at the deceased man. "The shot that hit him went all the way through his body too. The difference is that that bullet's path was through his heart, probably killed him instantly."

"That's unusual, both bullets going all the way through," Delgado commented.

"But not impossible," Detective Mendoza said. "Okay, let's figure out the angle of the shots and calculate where the slugs ended up."

Detective Sergeant Trueblood left his men to do their job. He walked forward and eyed Jacob Beam. Jace didn't need the medical examiner to tell him the man was dead. The surviving victim was already on a stretcher and being moved off the stage.

"Juan," Jace raised his voice. "Follow the stretcher out to the ambulance and see if the wounded guy can tell you where he was when he was shot. Ask if he had been standing or in some other position. That may give you an idea of where the shots came from."

Juan Mendoza gave a quick nod, moving swiftly.

Motioning to a nearby officer, Jace said, "I hear there was a witness who saw the shooter. Did we get a description sent to the station and forwarded to all available police personnel?"

"Yes, sir," Officer Clarkson replied. "We have police cars canvassing the streets and officers combing the immediate area."

Jace nodded. "Where's the witness?"

Before the cop could answer, Mibs interrupted. "Jace, I promised Mason I would take him to the hospital." She motioned to the man on the stretcher. "That's his father."

"Ah, sir." Clarkson pointed to Mibs, who had approached the stage. "She's the witness. She bumped into the killer fleeing the scene."

Jace's eyes widened. He stuffed down his concern and focused on the job. Jace straightened and put on his detective demeanor. "Mibs," he instructed. "I need you to stay here since you're a witness."

Mason stepped forward. The concern for his father pushed aside his usual apologetic manner. "But my dad...I want to go with my dad."

"It's okay," Jace assured him. "I'll have someone else drive you to the hospital." Scanning the auditorium, he spotted two patrol officers coming through the entrance. "Jameson and Harte!" he yelled. "Need you over here."

When they heard their names, the two patrolmen turned and headed over to the lead detective. "What do you need, sir?" Harte asked.

"Take this young man to the hospital and find out where they are treatin' his father–" Jace turned to the boy. "What's your dad's name?"

"Mike…Roberts."

"Harte, you take care of that. Make sure the boy is with someone responsible before you leave him."

"Jameson, I need you to stay here. I'll talk to you in a few minutes." Jace jumped off the stage and landed effortlessly in front of the seating area.

"Mibs." Jace guided her several feet away so the others waiting in the occupied seats were out of earshot. "So…you saw the shooter? How close were you? Do you think you could help our sketch artist draw a picture of him?"

"Yes, I believe I could help with that. Since he knocked me down, I had a good view of him."

"Knocked you down?" Jace pulled back to assess her. "Sweetheart, are you all right? Do you want to see a doctor?"

"I'm fine," Mibs said. "Really! I'm okay."

"You saw him clearly, but do you think he would recognize you?"

"Well…yeah." She shrugged. "Probably since the guy aimed a gun at me."

"What?" Jace growled. "He did *what?*"

Mibs lifted her hands. "It's okay. The guy didn't have time to pull the trigger because people ran through the doorway. I came in just as he rushed out from behind the curtain. I guess I jarred him, too. It took him a second to regain his balance. By then, voices and running feet were only a few feet away." Mibs shivered at the memory. "It happened so quickly; he turned and ran out the exit."

Jace mumbled under his breath as he turned to the waiting patrolman. "Jameson."

"Right here, Detective," he answered.

"From what Miss Monahan just told me, not only is she the only witness, but the shooter saw her face."

The patrolman gave his boss an understanding nod. "You want me to get her somewhere safe."

"Definitely! Take her to the police station, and have her work with our sketch artist. After that, let her go through the photos of known felons." Jace emphasized, "Don't let her out of your sight. Stay glued to her until I can get there, and *don't* let her leave."

"Yes, sir. I got it."

When Jace glanced back at Mibs, she frowned. "Sounds like you're putting me under lock and key." She wrapped her arms together. "Do you think this guy will come after me?"

"It's a genuine possibility." He took hold of her shoulders, scanning her eyes. "I'm not about to take any chances."

"I will be careful and take precautions. But, if you think that you're going to lock me away like some delicate flower...well, that's not going to happen." Mibs straightened.

Jace let out a deep sigh. "No, I guess not, considerin' whom I'm talkin' to." Squeezing her shoulders, he requested, "But, for now, please go with Officer Jameson. Stay at the station until I get there. Okay?"

After a moment's pause, she replied, "Okay."

"Detective Trueblood, it just dawned on me that Harte took the patrol car. Is there another vehicle available?" Jameson queried.

"How about mine?" Mibs suggested. "It's parked outside."

Jace nodded. "Jameson, before you leave the building, have two officers check the area, especially nearby roofs, and have someone pull the car up to the door."

Jace watched as the officer escorted Mibs out of the building before he pulled out his notebook and a pen to start interviewing the people waiting in the seats. Unless they had something significant to contribute, he intended to let them leave after taking their statements.

"Detective Trueblood." Officer Martha Schroeder moved down the aisle toward him. "We have several people outside who want to come in. They say their kids are in here."

"Better let them in. It's good if the parents are here because I don't want to interview the children without them. Have each claim their son or daughter and wait in the next empty row. Let them know we just want to ask if the kids saw anything." The officer turned. Jace stopped her. "Make sure that *only* the parents or guardians come in, no gawkers."

Over the next hour, the adults and children he talked with said they all heard the shots but didn't see anything. When two moms had realized that the loud bangs were gunshots, they'd grabbed their children and ran out the stage's side entrance to get them to safety. One of the frantic parents stated that she heard the back door bang shut but didn't see the fleeing suspect.

It was late afternoon before the interviews were completed. Everyone except Mrs. Barns, two theater board members, and police personnel had already left the building. The medical examiner had come and gone, and the body had been taken to the morgue. Jace tucked his notebook into his suit coat's inside pocket as he approached Mendoza and Delgado.

The lead detective stopped in front of the pair, putting his hands on his hips as he waited for their report.

Juan Mendoza cleared his throat. "We found the bullet that went through the dead man, Beam." As he shook his head from side to side, he added, "I'm pretty sure it's from a .38, but I don't think it will be traceable because it hit a metal post, and it's smashed flat."

"What about the one that passed through Roberts?" Jace asked. "I heard that it didn't hit any bones. Hopefully, it'll be intact; we can find a match on the ballistic ammo chart and determine what type of bullet was used. Maybe we'll be able to match it to a bullet or gun from another crime."

Delgado shrugged. "We haven't been able to find it yet." He pointed to the north end of the stage. "From what we can determine, the shooter fired from behind those stage props. Since no one saw him out front, he probably snuck behind the curtain to hide his coming and going. That coincides with the witness saying that he rushed out from behind the curtain at the other end.

"Well, it has to be here! Keep canvassing the area," Jace demanded. Hearing a low rumble from Juan Mendoza's stomach, Jace stopped and scanned his detectives' faces. "You guys haven't had lunch, have you?"

Juan raised his eyebrow and shook his head.

Jace dropped his hands to his sides and signaled Juan and Gene to follow him. "Come on. I'll buy you guys a sandwich." He motioned to the Havendale forensic team investigating the stage. "They can handle things until you two get back."

Chapter 19

When Jace returned to his office at the Havendale Police Station, Mibs was sitting at his desk, carefully staring at pages of an album containing pictures of known criminals. Jace took a moment to watch his pretty girlfriend. Considering her independent nature, the detective doubted he could convince Mibs to stay at a safe house. But he still planned on having security around her when he couldn't be by her side.

"Anyone seem familiar?" Jace asked.

Mibs jumped at his words. "Oh! Hi, Jace. I didn't hear you come in. No, none of these people are the man I saw run out of the community theater." She turned the last page, carefully scrutinized the photos, and sighed. "Nope, not here. And this is the last book."

Jace placed a cup of coffee on his desk and handed a second one to Mibs. "Three creams, correct?"

"Yes, thank you!"

Jace plopped down in his swivel chair and leaned back, running his hand through his hair. "Hmm. No one recognized the description you gave, and the shooter isn't in our books of known felons. Sounds like the gunman isn't from around here. And he doesn't sound like a seasoned professional."

Mibs remained silent.

"I need to go to the hospital and talk to Mike

166

Roberts." Jace pushed his chair back and stood up. "You prefer to stay here until I get back, or do you want to go with me?"

"Go *with* you. Mike is a friend."

~~

Michael Roberts had gone through surgery to repair the entrance and exit wounds the bullet had made when it tore through his right shoulder. He was sore but grateful to be alive. The shot had missed any vital organs and bones. Because of weakness from the blood loss, the doctor recommended that he spend the night in the hospital. If everything were good in the morning, he would be released.

Mason was curled up in a big chair in the hospital room; an empty food bag and soda container were on the windowsill next to him.

Mike smiled at his son before he nodded off.

~~

After knocking, Jace and Mibs entered Mike's hospital room. The father and son both appeared to be asleep. As the detective stepped closer, he noticed that Roberts' eyelids were slit open a fraction of an inch, revealing that even prone in a hospital bed, the former military man kept a watch over himself and especially his son.

"Hello, Detective Trueblood," the patient mumbled.

"How are you doing, Mr. Roberts?" Knowing that he had never met the man, Jace assumed Roberts had seen him at the crime scene.

"Getting there." Mike puckered his mouth.

"Hi, Mike," said Mibs. "You need a drink?" As soon as he nodded, she picked up the cup and straw, sitting on the small dresser near his bed. Holding the straw to his lips, she waited for him to take several large sips before setting the cup aside.

"Thanks, Mibs." He glanced at his sleeping son before clearing his throat. Mike stared at Jace. "I recognize you from the picture Mibs showed me on her phone. Are you here officially?"

Jace took out his identification and held it up so Mr. Roberts could see it. "Yes, I am. I know that Officer Harte talked to you, but I need to ask a few more questions."

"Dad?" Mason sat up, blinking several times.

"Everything is fine, son," Michael said. "Miss Monahan is here, and this is Detective Trueblood. The detective is going to ask some questions."

Jace studied the boy. "Do you mind if I ask you a few questions before I talk to your dad?"

Michael nodded to his son.

"Yes, sir," Mason said. "What do you want to know?"

Softening his voice, Jace said, "I'm asking everyone who was at the theater during the time of the shooting what they saw and heard. Anything, even if it doesn't seem important.

Did you see any strangers? Anyone who didn't seem to belong there?"

Mason frowned. "I'd been standing near my dad. He helped me learn my stage spots and how I needed to move around during the play. I didn't see any strangers. I heard the gunshots, but it didn't seem like anything important." The ten-year-old boy's lips scrunched together before he took a shallow breath and continued talking. "I saw Dad jerk. He made a grunting sound, and I saw a red spot spreading across his shirt." Mason started to shake.

Mibs inched closer to him, picked up his hand and held it tightly.

"I'm sorry you went through that." Jace crouched down in front of the young man. "Thank you for talkin' to me."

Mason nodded.

Straightening, Jace motioned to Mibs. "Why don't you take Mason to the waiting room while I speak to Mr. Roberts? Officer Jameson is in the hall; he'll stay with you."

After Mibs and Mason left the room, Jace stepped toward the hospital bed.

Mike asked, "Detective, would you mind passing me the control for this bed?"

The combination call button and up/down switch had slipped down the side of the mattress. Pulling it out, Jace handed it to Mike.

The man flinched as he adjusted the top of the bed. "Okay, Detective, ask away."

Jace pulled out a notebook and pen. "Walk me through what happened, from your perspective."

"At the time, I had been paying more attention to helping Mason learn his cues and places than anything off stage. My son and I had just passed behind Jacob Beam. We headed to the center of the stage, and Jacob walked toward the Emerald City set. I heard the gunshots. Two in close succession. Sounded like a .38 revolver. My first instinct was to grab Mason and pull him down." A mixture of anger and dismay flitted across his features as the father recalled the incident. "He was too far away for me to reach him, and getting hit stunned me for a moment. All I could do was yell at Mason to *hit the deck*." Michael winced. "By then, the shooting had stopped. I suspected that the shots came from the north end of the stage. I steadied myself and scanned the area but didn't see anyone. Jacob was down and bleeding, and people started screaming and ducking behind things." Michael stopped talking.

"You said it sounded like a .38. I take it you're familiar with that type of handgun?"

"After over twenty years in service, I can identify almost any firearm you put in front of me and how it sounds."

"Next question." Jace paused for a second, turning a page in his notebook. "Who do you think the target was? Beam, you, or any available person?"

"I have no reason to believe it was me and can't think of anyone who'd want me dead. I'm pretty sure the bullet I caught was because I was behind Beam."

"You think the shooter targeted Jacob Beam?"

"I don't know. I'm just saying I doubt if I was the target, and I would guess if it were a random shooting, the shots wouldn't have been so close together."

Jace slowly nodded. "Okay, so nobody has a beef against you. Unhappy with you?"

"Well..." Michael hesitated. "As far as not being happy with me...I doubt if I'm on my ex-wife's friends' list. But I don't think she would take a shot at me, especially since Mason was nearby. I don't believe Shelia has ever held a gun, much less knows how to use one. Besides, as far as I know, she doesn't have any idea that we're living in Havendale now."

"Okay," Jace said. "Just to cover all the bases, can you give me her address?"

"Yeah. It's in my address book at home. You can have someone go over there if you need it now, or if tomorrow is soon enough, I'll call you after I get home."

"Tomorrow should be fine." Jace slid his notebook back into his pocket.

Jace stepped into the hallway outside Michael's room. Sergeant Brice Long waited for him. Long maintained the chain of command, took care of special reports and numerous forms, took calls, and relayed needed information to patrol cars.

"Brice." Jace gave his associate a nod. "You have something for me?"

"Yep." The sergeant handed him a folder. "It appears that Beam was a high-priced divorce lawyer. Those are copies of threatening letters, seven of them over the last ten years."

After scanning the information in the folder, Jace whistled. "I'd say Jacob Beam had a few enemies. I see three different names to go with these seven letters."

"The last four letters are the most recent and from the same person," Long stated. "Guy named Samuel Hannity; he wasn't happy with the results of the divorce settlement Beam won for his ex."

"Hmm," Trueblood mumbled. "Has anyone from the department talked to these people yet?"

"Not yet. I just got this information. I tried to talk to his wife, but she was not in any shape for an interview."

Jace frowned. "The little girl, the daughter...it had to be rough on her to see her father shot."

Long just nodded.

Checking his watch, Jace realized that Long should have been off duty by now. "Don't you need to get home to your kids?"

"Cassandra doesn't have volleyball practice tonight. She'll keep an eye on the other two and give me a call if anything is needed."

"She's a good kid," Jace emphasized. "How old is she now?'

"Fifteen," Brice answered. "She's been extra helpful lately because she started driver's ed; lots of hints about getting a car next year." He chuckled.

Long had lost his wife, Madison, over five years ago. Cassandra had been barely ten years old; Nicolas, nine; and Matthew, seven when their mom died of breast cancer. On more than one occasion, Brice had declared how lucky he was that Madison's mom had stepped in to help the grieving family. Brice had done an excellent job as a single dad, but there had been a few more challenges this past year after losing his mother-in-law to a heart attack.

"If you don't have to head home, could you get started on the people in this folder? First thing, see if any of them match the sketch we have of the shooter. Then, find out where each of them was this mornin'."

"Will, do."

"See you later." Jace gave Brice a half-wave as he headed toward the waiting room to tell Mason that he could go back to be with his dad.

Chapter 20

Jace decided to wait until the following day before talking to the murdered man's wife. He sent Officer Jameson home and headed to Monahan's Sewing Shop with Mibs.

"I figured that you'd called your aunt and told her you'd been delayed." Jace started his truck and checked his rearview mirror before pulling out of the parking space.

"Yes." Mibs clicked the latch on her seatbelt. "Aunt Bernie is heating a pre-made lasagna in the microwave and waiting for me to get home." Leaning back in the seat and closing her eyes, she mumbled, "Will you be able to stay and eat with us?"

"I'll grab a bite, but then I have to head back to the station. Besides this shooting, we're still working on the hit-and-run case."

"How's that going? Do you have any solid leads?"

Jace pursed his lips. "We have a pretty good idea of who drove the car, but I want to follow up on a few more things before we bring the suspected driver in." He sighed. "I think it may be a case of a new driver who panicked and took off instead of staying at the scene. I hate the idea of two young lives being messed up – the accident victim and the teen driver."

When they reached Mibs' combination shop and home, Jace walked around to the passenger's door of his Silverado and took her hand as she climbed out of the truck. "I'll get the door," he said, pulling out the key, which Mibs had given him in case of an emergency. As they entered the back entrance, the Belgian Malinois greeted them with a wagging tail.

They made their way into the small kitchenette situated between the shop and Bernice's living area. The spicey aroma from the lasagna filled the air.

Mibs gave her aunt a gentle hug. "Sorry I took so long to get home. Did everything go okay for you, Deanna, and Mary today?"

"We did fine. The store is all closed up. I was just worried about you." She narrowed her eyes. "Are you sure you're all right?"

"It's been a tough day, but I haven't taken time to let myself think about it yet." Mibs grabbed a pair of oven gloves, opened the microwave, and pulled out their dinner. "Let's sit down and eat. I want to relax for a few minutes before Jace returns to work."

Bernie had also warmed up garlic bread to go with the lasagna. The scent made Jace's mouth water. The three of them ate quietly for several minutes.

Jace hadn't realized how hungry he was until he took his first bite of cheesy lasagna, cleared off his plate, and wolfed down a second piece of bread before he sat back.

"Thank you for dinner, Bernie. I always appreciate you having a place for me at your table."

"You know you're always welcome to join us." Bernie's softly wrinkled face gazed fondly at Jace.

Mibs set her fork and knife across her empty plate. "Okay, now that we've had some food, shall we talk about what needs to be done? Will we have a police car stationed outside the shop? After the last time, I had hoped we would never need security following us around again." During the previous year, a vicious attack on Mibs' best friend had led the police to assign a security detail to watch over the Monahans. Jace knew that the protection had been both reassuring and aggravating for Mibs.

Jace rested his elbows on the table and laced his fingers together as he frowned at the two ladies. "Mibs, I'd rather assign security and not need it than ignore the possibility that the shooter may try to eliminate you as a witness."

A pained expression crossed Bernie's face, but the aged woman remained silent.

Mibs sat back with a resigned expression and nodded. "I hope they find this guy quickly."

"Sweetheart, I do too." Jace stood and pulled out his cell phone. "I have a feeling that the assailant is more likely to watch for you when you're out rather than here at the store. But I'm still going to see who's available tonight and have them stationed outside."

"Wait! Can I go back to the community theater and get the costume we're working on for Wally, one of the young actors? I suppose they may cancel the play because of what happened, but for the sake of the kids who have been putting in so much work, I hope they don't."

Jace slipped the phone back into his pocket. "I planned on going back over there to see if the crime scene techs have finished up. As long as it's in an area they've already cleared, it should be okay. I'll take you with me, then bring you back here."

He turned to Bernie. "I don't think this guy will have any interest in you, but I can have someone stay with you if you'd like."

"No, I'm not worried about being here. I agree; the killer has no reason to target me." Pointing to the dog lying quietly nearby, Bernie said, "Leave Shadow here. I feel more secure with her. She'll let me know if anyone is around."

Jace knelt down to rub the canine between the ears. "Shadow, you stay here with the girls again tonight."

"I'll be back later." Mibs hugged her aunt before turning and reaching for Jace's hand. "Can I bring my car back here from the theater? The officer who escorted me to the police station drove it back there."

Jace hesitated, to give the question some consideration. Then he slowly agreed. "I'll follow you as you drive back home. But, Mibs, I don't want you driving anywhere by yourself until this killer is apprehended. You must allow one of my officers to drive you or at least have them follow your car if you absolutely have to go somewhere."

"I think you'd feel better if I were secluded in a safe room somewhere." Mibs' brows furrowed.

Sighing, Jace quipped, "You got that right, darlin'."

When Jace and Mibs entered the community theater, they found the senior crime scene technician, Todd Benson, and his team preparing to lock things up and leave for the night. Delgado and Mendoza had already gone to the station to help Sergeant Long follow up on the suspects from Beam's threatening letters. Other than the sketch Mibs had helped to create, no one had retrieved any factual evidence to identify the person who had killed Jacob Beam and wounded Michael Roberts.

"You didn't find the bullet slug that passed through Roberts?" the lead detective grilled the forensic specialists. "It couldn't have disappeared."

Signaling for Jace to follow him, Benson led him to the thick maroon curtain hanging at the edge of the stage and pointed out a small hole near the bottom of the material. "That's a bullet hole. I'd say the slug went through the material and kept going. But heck if I know where it went!" The technician pointed to the floor. "Following the calculated direction, the slug should have ended up right here. Besides visually searching, I asked the guys to run a metal detector across the floor and even up the wall."

Jace crossed his arms as he studied the area in question, hoping for a possible clue as to where the missing slug went.

~~

Mibs had been listening to the conversation as she wandered around the room, searching for the container that held the unfinished costumes. She saw the edge of the tub protruding from the doorway of the far dressing room. Walking closer, she realized that her basket of sewing notions had been moved and placed on top of the costume container. It dawned on her where she had left that particular basket just as she noticed a small, round hole in its side.

Turning toward the investigators, she swallowed and cleared her throat. "Jace." He didn't respond, so she raised her voice, "Jace, would you guys come here, please?"

The tone in Mibs' voice must have caught his attention; with a few quick steps, Jace reached her side. "Is something wrong? What is it?"

Blinking a few times, Mibs pointed to her sewing items. "Someone moved my basket. It was probably Anita Barns trying to be helpful." She pointed to the side of the basket.

"There's a hole right here. My notions may have the evidence of the murder—the evidence you're hunting for."

Benson, who had followed Jace, asked, "Do you understand what she's talking about? What do her notions have to do with the murder?"

Eyeing the basket, the edge of Jace's lip curved up in a half-smile. "She doesn't mean notions as in *ideas*. I've been hanging around this seamstress long enough to know what notions are." Jace turned to the technician. "They're small sewing items, like pins and buttons, and apparently, that's what's in this basket."

"Okay?" Benson shook his head. "And?"

Placing his hand on Mibs' shoulder, Jace asked, "Mibs, do you remember where the basket had been placed?"

"Oh, yes. I know precisely where I left it." Mibs started to reach for the handle but abruptly stopped. "Do you want me to put it back where it was?"

"Please do, exactly where you last saw it."

Benson let out a gasp when he saw her carry the basket over to the curtain and place the back of it in front of the small bullet hole.

"You still have gloves on, Todd?" Jace gestured for Benson to come forward. "I think you may find your bullet now."

The crime scene technician's mouth fell open. Then he shook his head, opened the lid of the basket, and had his assistant take pictures as he carefully examined inside. It didn't take long for him to find the missing slug, still in good shape; it was lodged in a package of half-inch elastic.

"Get it to the crime lab right away," Jace told Benson. "I'll talk to you tomorrow."

He put one arm around Mibs and used the other to carry the tub of costumes she indicated. Jace reminded her, "You know this isn't the first time you've helped find an important clue in a murder investigation."

Chewing on her lower lip, Mibs remembered the thread of evidence she had spotted at a previous crime scene at the sisters' mansion. She responded in a quiet voice, "Glad to be of help, Detective."

Chuckling, Jace walked her out of the building.

When they reached her shop, Jace followed Mibs' car into the parking lot behind the building, and pulled to a stop. He got out of his truck, retrieved the costume container from her car, carried it to the back door, and set it down. When Mibs opened her small wristlet purse to find her key, Jace stopped her.

"Let's wait in my vehicle until the night security gets here." He pulled out his cell phone. After making arrangements for a patrol car to keep watch overnight, he put the phone away. Jace opened the driver's-side door of his Silverado and gave her a hand up into the cab. "The security detail will be here in less than fifteen minutes."

"I'm sure I'll be fine if you need to get back to the station."

"Getting back to the station can wait a bit. I want to stay here with you, even if it is only for a few minutes." Jace climbed into the seat next to her, then closed the truck door.

Mibs noticed his troubled expression. "Is that frown because you're worried about me?"

"Do you think I shouldn't be when that shooter could still be close by?"

Crossing her arms, she sat back. "You risk your life every day, just like every police officer or first responder does. When you're on the job, you never know when someone might choose you for a target. Don't you think *that* worries me?"

"I know it does, and I'm sorry, Mibs," Jace said. "But I chose this career and all the challenges that come with it. I've trained for all kinds of situations, so you don't need to worry so much." Sliding closer, he put his arms around her. "Let's talk about something else in the little time left before the squad car gets here."

Mibs gazed into his intense eyes and whispered, "Did you have something in mind?"

Nodding, Jace murmured, "Uh-huh." Gently running his thumb across the top of her lip, then cradling her face in his hands, he leaned down and kissed her. Mibs felt the warmth of his kiss spread through her body. A starburst of joy exploded in her mind, and a feeling of softly fluttering butterflies filled her stomach.

Chapter 21

The following day, Jace had called the Havendale Police Station before leaving his house. The ballistics report on the slug found at the community theater wasn't in yet. So far, nothing concrete had been discovered to implicate any suspects who had sent threatening letters to Jacob Beam.

Detectives Mendoza and Delgado had informed him that they'd used the information that Sergeant Long had given them to track down the letter writers. One disgruntled person, Jerome Blanche, had written a letter over eight years ago. After some research, Long had located Blanche serving time in prison for theft. The check on his correspondence had not revealed anything that would indicate he'd hired someone on the outside to attack Beam. That information, along with the fact that he had been remarried and divorced twice since his first marriage, made him an unlikely suspect.

According to Mendoza and Delgado, the second person who had threatened Jacob Beam was a woman who now lived out of state. It had been four years since Rita Hammond's angry letter was sent. Mendoza and Delgado had interviewed her, coming away with the sense that she had moved on. Nevertheless, they'd checked out her alibi for the day of the shooting. They'd also obtained a warrant to have a member of their tech team review her online activities. After finding nothing suspicious, the detectives were ready to check her off the suspect list.

They had not yet located Samuel Hannity. Up until six months ago, he had lived at an address in Havendale. Now, he seemed to have dropped off the face of the earth. They were still researching, checking for a change of address, and had contacted the DMV for vehicle information changes. So far, no luck. The detectives had talked to his ex-wife, Monica. She'd informed them that a restraining order was in effect. Samuel Hannity had continued to harass Monica after the divorce until she'd sought help from the police. She hadn't heard from him or seen him since the order was issued several months ago. Because of Hannity's continued antagonistic attitude and apparent disappearance, the suspicions about him were increasing.

Jace would get more details when he reached the station. The frustration of not finding answers made him even more determined to uncover the perpetrator and investigate the reason for the shooting.

After adjusting his tie, he decided to take a few minutes to stop and say good morning to his girlfriend. He backed his Silverado out of the driveway, then drove the short distance. As he turned onto the side street next to the sewing shop, Jace waved at the parked police car on security duty. When he pulled into the back lot of Monahan's, he saw Mibs just inside the half-open back door. It appeared she'd let Shadow outside. Jace was glad she'd stayed in the building instead of accompanying the dog into the lot. He watched Shadow staring up at a blue jay as it made a loud 'jeer' sound for anyone who might be listening. The dog trotted to Jace's truck and waited for him to get out. After acknowledging Shadow with a rub behind the ears, he turned to Mibs.

Calling from inside the doorway, she gave him a cheery greeting. "Hi, Jace! Isn't it beautiful today? The sky is so blue!"

"Yeah, it's nice. And not quite as hot either." Jace thought of how most of July had been in the nineties, making this morning's seventy degrees enjoyable. He pulled out a small orange ball that he'd hidden in his pocket and showed it to Shadow. "You want to play, girl?"

The dog's tail wagged as she responded with a bark.

Tossing the ball toward the grassy area across the lot, Jace joined Mibs. "Willy's daughter sent a box of items for Shadow. It included several of these orange balls. I'll leave one here if you like."

"Sure. Maybe stopping to play catch with Shadow will force me to take a break once in a while, too."

"Ah...for now, just toss it to her in the back room. I don't want you spending unnecessary time out in the open."

Mibs' only response was to frown.

"By the way, the sixteen-year-old that we were planning to bring in for questioning about the hit and run turned himself in," Jace informed Mibs. "He'd been feeling so guilty that he couldn't stay quiet any longer. It's what we suspected: a scared, new, young driver. I'm hoping the judge will be lenient with him since he's never been in trouble before. It should help that the victim is going to recover."

"I hope he and the girl will both make it through without too great an impact on their futures. Terrible thing for both."

After throwing the ball a few more times and praising the dog, Jace headed inside.

"Do you have time for coffee and a cinnamon roll?" Mibs asked.

"I'll take a cup to go. Your coffee is a lot better than the brew in our breakroom." He watched as Mibs filled a travel mug. "Maybe I can take a few hours off on Sunday morning."

"We usually go to 8:00 a.m. Mass and should be home before 9:30." Glancing over her shoulder, Mibs asked, "Why don't you come to church with us? I know you said that you haven't attended since your first year of college, but maybe you could think about coming back."

Jace tried to stop the frown before it came, to no avail.

~~

Mibs was surprised *and* upset when she saw the irritation on Jace's face. She shook her head. "You told me that you stopped going to church after your brother, Connor, died, but that was over twelve years ago."

"I know exactly how long it's been!" He took a deep breath and continued, "Do you think that I should forget about him because time has passed?"

"I never mentioned anything about forgetting Connor." Mibs' instinct was to reach out and put her arms around Jace, but her intuition cautioned her against that action. He didn't want sympathy. "That doesn't mean you have to stay angry forever, stay away from the Church, from God's house, for the rest of your life."

"God's house!" Jace huffed. "Why would I want to go to one of God's earthly houses when I've never had the opportunity to go to my brother's? Connor would have been thirty this year. He'd likely have had his own home by now, probably even a family, maybe kids. But he never will because God let him die!" Backing away from Mibs, he crossed his arms and shook his head. "Can't you understand why I've lost my faith?"

Mibs studied the man in front of her. "You're mad at God, but you haven't lost your faith."

"What's that supposed to mean?"

"You can't be furious with God—unless you believe in His existence." Mibs regarded Jace with tenderness, wishing she had a way to lessen the bitter resentment in his heart. "It hurts when we lose someone we love, because we miss them. But we should remember that our souls belong to God, and He has a right to call us back to Heaven, any one of us, whenever *He* wishes—even the ones we are closest to."

"Okay, Mibs." Jace took a deep breath and slowly let it out before grudgingly offering, "If it means so much to you, I'll go to church with you."

That statement wasn't what she wanted to hear. "I don't want you to go to church just because you're trying to placate me. It needs to be *your* decision. All I ask is that you think about what I said."

They stood in the small kitchen area, staring at each other for several long moments. Jace finally turned away, saying, "I have to get to the station." He left without another word or a backward glance.

Mibs turned back to the counter as tears slipped down her cheeks. Finally, wiping them away, she picked up the coffee Jace had left and drank it down without adding her usual cream. She heard a soft whine and realized that Shadow was right behind her. The perceptive canine sensed the sadness that had settled in the room. Kneeling down, Mibs wrapped her arms around the dog's neck, finding comfort in the animal's presence.

"Are you okay, dear?" Aunt Bernie watched from the doorway.

Mibs lifted her chin and nodded. "I guess so." She stood up and approached her aunt. She tried to smile; instead, tears filled her eyes again. "I guess you heard everything. Oh, Aunt Bernie, I said all the wrong things! I shouldn't have said anything."

Aunt Bernie looped her arm through Mibs' and guided her to the chairs in the breakroom. "My dear girl, the subject of faith needed to come up because it's an important part of your life. If you and your young man are going to have a lasting relationship, you *must* discuss it." Patting the girl's hand, she added, "And if this hurt in his heart has been smoldering all these years, he probably needs to talk about it, too."

Mibs was polite and helpful to the customers who needed her assistance during the day, letting Deanna and Mary wait on anyone who didn't specifically need her expertise. The upsetting exchange with Jace that morning had left her in a quiet and pensive mood. Instead of passing Wally's costume back to Deanna, she decided to make the requested changes herself. As she sewed on the fake-fur material, she kept darting a glance to her phone, hoping Jace would call.

He didn't call her, but he phoned the shop's number. Mary answered and relayed the message that he would leave Shadow with

Aunt Bernie and Mibs again tonight. The day seemed to drag. After the shop closed, Mibs ate a little supper before staying up late, sitting in front of the television, channel surfing without really watching with interest. Sleep didn't come easy that night; it was well past midnight before Mibs finally drifted off.

She woke early and made up her mind that today would be a good day. She started with a hearty breakfast. Mibs hit Bernie's number on her speed dial and asked her to set the table for two; she would be bringing down French toast and cheesy, scrambled eggs. The ladies shared the meal and talked about sewing, shopping, and movies. Shadow sat next to the table, eyes roving between the two women as they spoke.

By the time the door to the shop was unlocked, Mibs had a smile on her face.

The happy demeanor would satisfy customers, but her aunt would likely know that her smile was superficial.

Late that afternoon, the phone rang.

"Hello, Tony. How are you?" Mibs heard her aunt's greeting. After Aunt Bernie hung up, she informed Mibs that Tony planned to bring over a Brother's wide-table sewing and quilting machine. "He said that a customer had purchased it, thinking that she would find time to learn quilting. It hadn't been removed from the box in years, so she decided it was just taking up space and gathering dust. Tony bought it for a fraction of its worth. He asked if we would be interested in it. I told him yes, so he'll be here sometime between 5:00 and 6:00." Aunt Bernie leaned in close to Mibs. "You've talked about getting a better quilting machine, so I didn't think it would hurt to check it out."

"Definitely! It sounds like something we can use." Mibs nodded. "Did he say how much he wanted for it?"

"No, but I'm sure Tony will give us a reasonable price."

"That's true." Mibs glanced up. No customers were in the store, so she grabbed the orange ball and spent several minutes in the storage room playing with Shadow, trying to keep her thoughts away from Jace.

Chapter 22

Slightly before 5:30 p.m., the bell for the back buzzer sounded. Mibs opened the door to find Tony Vitali smiling down at her, the sun silhouetting his tall frame and highlighting his raven-black hair. "Hey, Wonderful, do you want to come and examine the sewing machine? It's in the trunk of my car."

Even though she expected Tony, Mibs gave her friend a half-hearted smile when she saw that it was him and not Jace. Despite her act of cheerfulness, the hope of her boyfriend calling had lingered in her mind all day. "Sounds like a good idea."

As she stepped out of the building, Mibs waved at the policeman parked across the street, letting him know that there was no threat from the dark-haired man walking beside her.

The officer nodded.

"What's that about?" Tony glanced over her shoulder toward the police cruiser.

"I'll tell you when we get inside." Mibs sighed.

Tony led the way to his car, an indigo blue Dodge Challenger SRT Demon.

"This is a lot different than the truck you were driving the last time you were here," Mibs observed. "Beautiful vehicle."

"This is what I use for business and just for fun. The truck is for hauling things for the shop. I also have a 1949 Buick Super, a two-door classic car, which I enjoy tinkering with in my garage. I'll have to give you a ride in it sometime."

"I'd like that," Mibs answered without much enthusiasm as she ran a hand along the smooth hood of the Challenger, still warm from the drive.

"Mirabelle." Tony stepped closer and placed his hands on her shoulders. "What's wrong? And don't say *nothing*. Does it have something to do with that cop who's watching?"

"No. That's something else."

"Mibs, tell me! Why does it seem like you're about to cry?"

Trembling lips proceeded the tears that slipped from half-closed lids. "Oh, Tony, I fought with Jace yesterday. He hasn't called or come by. I guess I shouldn't have said what I did."

"Come here, friend." Tony pulled Mibs into his arms and patted her back as she explained the verbal clash she'd had with her guy. After explaining what she and Jace had bumped heads about, Mibs mumbled, "Should I keep my thoughts to myself about my beliefs?"

Tony chuckled. "I don't think you could if you tried. I remember when we were young kids, and I missed Mass one Sunday because I wanted to finish a computer game. You wouldn't come out and shoot basketball hoops with me until I knelt down and said an Our Father to make up for missing church."

"Did I really do that?"

"Oh, yeah!" Tony hugged her tighter. "And I love you for being who you are."

~~

"What the heck are you doing holding my girlfriend?" a deep voice growled. "Mibs, what's going on here?" Jace greeted her with a combined tone of anger and hurt.

Mibs started to move away, but the man pulled her back. The man calmly stated, "I'll hold Mirabelle anytime she needs me."

"Well, she doesn't need you!" Jace stepped forward, placed his hands around Mibs' waist, and lifted her out of Tony's arms, setting her by the side of the car. Moving closer, he stood face to face with the other man. "I asked what's going on!"

The man grabbed the front of Jace's shirt, twisting the material along with the tie. "What's going on is that I'm trying to decide whether or not I should punch you in the mouth for making her cry."

Jace clutched the front of the other man's shirt, giving it a hard tug. Before he could make another comment, Mibs grabbed Jace's arm and pulled.

"Jace Trueblood and Tony Vitali, stop right now!"

This time the other man released his hold on Jace. He grasped Mibs' shoulders and moved her back. "Stay out of the way, Mibs."

"Ugh!" She threw up her arms and stomped toward the building. As she headed toward the door, the Havendale police officer exited his cruiser.

Officer Brett Clarkson leaned forward, ready to head across the street. Jace held up his hand, indicating that the patrolman should stay away. Jace's shoulders slumped. He quietly asked the man—whom he realized must be Mibs' childhood friend, Tony—"Did she tell you I made her cry?"

"She didn't have to tell me. I saw her tears. That's why I was comforting her," Tony stated. "Mibs told me what upset her. I know Mirabelle's zeal concerning her faith, so I can see why she finds that upsetting."

The barely two-inch difference in their heights made it easy for the two men to stare into each other's eyes, steely stares mirroring back and forth between them.

"My first thought was to tell you to get out of her life, but for some reason, she cares about you." Tony leaned back and crossed his arms. "Personally, I think you're an *idiota!*"

Jace gave him a searing glare before he smiled with gritted teeth. "I don't speak Italian, but I get your point. And I know a few choice words for a guy who steps in between a couple when they're trying to work out their problems."

"So, are you saying that you'd fight for Mibs?"

"Whatever it takes! I don't want to lose her."

Tony nodded. "Okay, Trueblood, that makes

a difference. Mirabelle doesn't have a dad or brother around...but she has me. She's as close as I'll ever get to a sister, and I won't stand by and watch her cry. So, I'll only tell you once—don't hurt her!"

"I don't want her hurt either," Jace said and then paused. "Wait! Did you just say...sister? I thought..."

"I know what you thought, *idiota*. Now let me ask you something; do you think that you're the only one who's ever lost a loved one? I lost my mom when I was eight years old and my dad when I was in college. And I never had the pleasure of growing up with a brother. What about Mibs? She never knew either of her parents." Stepping closer to Jace, he added, "Stop feeling sorry for yourself and try being thankful that you had your kid brother for as long as you did."

As Jace stared at Tony, an unspoken truce grew between the two men. Tony turned away and walked to the back of his car, popping open the Challenger's trunk.

"Vitali," Jace called.

Tony peered over the top of the trunk, "What, Trueblood?"

"I'll think about what you said."

"Good." Tony hefted the box out from the trunk. "Now, why don't you make yourself useful? Close this trunk, and open the door to the shop for me."

~~

Mibs had stormed into the store and found

Aunt Bernie sitting on the couch in the break area perusing a magazine. Moving around the small table, she plopped down. "Aunt Bernie, Jace and Tony are arguing!" Gulping loudly, she said, "I'm worried they're going to hit each other!"

Aunt Bernie asked, "What upset them?"

"Ah! I think Jace got the wrong idea when he came outside and saw Tony's arms around me. He pulled me away from Tony and wanted to know what was going on." Mibs muttered, "I...tried to tell him...then Tony moved me away...neither would listen!" She crossed her arms and slumped back on the cushion with a *humph,* then shook her head. "I gave up and came inside."

"Hmm, I see." Aunt Bernie didn't seem too disturbed. "Probably best that you came in, my dear."

"But what if they actually start fighting? I mean, physically!"

Aunt Bernie patted Mibs' arm. "They're pretty evenly matched."

"What?" Mibs' mouth fell open at Bernie's calm demeanor.

"Well, Jace has police training, not just in the use of weapons, but also hand-to-hand combat. From what Tony has told me, he's not only proficient at fencing but also has a red belt in Taekwondo. They both should be able to hold their own."

Mibs' mouth remained open. "What?"

"Oh, don't worry. Those boys may jostle

each other around a bit, but they aren't going to be pulling out weapons," Aunt Bernie told Mibs before picking up her magazine and turning the page.

Mibs shook her head, moved from the couch to the floor, and put her arms around Shadow. She refused to watch the two men fighting. The dog licked the girl's face, possibly sensing her need for comfort.

It was a good five minutes before the door opened. Jace walked in, closely followed by Tony.

"Where would you like me to put this machine, Aunt Bernie?" Tony questioned.

"Just inside the shop, the first table on the right, please, Anthony." Aunt Bernie grabbed her cane and scooted to the front of the couch cushion.

Jace stepped closer and offered his arm to aid her in standing.

"Thank you, Jace," she said, steadying her cane. "I see you've met Anthony."

He wrinkled his brow. "Yes, we've met."

Mibs had scanned the faces of the men as they came in, searching for signs of fighting.

"I'll go examine the new quilting sewing machine," Aunt Bernie declared as she moved to the shop area.

"Mibs, may I talk with you? Please?" Jace offered his hand.

After a moment, Mibs accepted his hand. She stood, led him into her barely-larger-than-a-closet office, then closed the door. She leaned against the desk with a questioning expression and waited.

Jace's gaze lingered on her eyes. "Mibs, I'm sorry I raised my voice yesterday. I should never have taken my anger out on you." He stepped closer but kept his arms to his sides. "Can you forgive me?"

"Of course, I can; I do," she replied. "I'm sorry, too. I should have kept my thoughts to myself."

"No. Don't say that. I don't want you to hesitate to tell me anything, especially if it's important to you." He glanced away as embarrassment tinged his face. He cleared his throat. "Mibs, I'm even more sorry for the way I acted outside a few minutes ago."

"Flying off the handle like that is rather out of character for you," Mibs frowned. "I thought you trusted me."

"I do! Completely!"

Jace rubbed the back of his neck. "I think working undercover, then worrying about you being stalked by a killer has me on edge." Jace sighed. "But that's no excuse. I apologize. I really *am* sorry."

Jace slowly lifted his arms and held them open.

Mibs stepped into his embrace.

"Mibs, I've been doing a lot of thinking since yesterday."

She tilted her head up.

He explained, "You're right. If I go back to church, it needs to be because I want to, not because someone asked me. No matter how much I want to please them...please you..." He touched his forehead to hers. "I have a lot to wrap my head around."

"I can be patient," Mibs declared, then added, "if I try."

This brought a chuckle from Jace before he leaned back a few more inches and gazed down at her. "Mibs, there's one thing that I'm very sure about, without any doubt." He took a deep breath. "Mirabelle Louise Monahan, I've fallen in love with you."

She smiled, and her heart skipped as she responded, "Jace Ezekiel Trueblood, I love you, too."

Jace sighed. Pulling her closer, he rested his chin on her head. "That's very good to know."

Jace and Mibs made their way to the front of the store a few minutes later and found Tony working with the new sewing machine.

Aunt Bernie leaned forward, watching as he positioned a double-folded piece of material under the pressure foot. "Anthony is demonstrating some of the stitches on this machine," she explained. "The variety of designs is quite extensive."

Tony glanced up as the couple entered the room. "From the goofy grins the two of you are wearing, I'm guessing you made up." He pressed the pedal that ran a line of fancy stitches along the cloth. He lifted the pressure foot, snipped the thread, and held up the material. Tony tossed it to Mibs. "What do you think?"

Mibs studied the dozen unique stitch designs and was impressed. "Very nice! These stitches will dress up a quilted piece."

Pushing the chair back, Tony moved away from the table, presenting the sewing machine with the added quilting functions. "It's all yours, Wonderful."

"Terrific. I love it." She turned. "I'll get the checkbook. Just tell me how much we owe you."

"I don't suppose you'd let me give it to you?" Tony offered.

"Of course not. You're running a business. How will you make money if you keep giving things away?" Mibs softly punched him on the arm.

"I have enough money." He paused. "In fact, I just accepted a job with a well-known company to update their software with state-of-the-art safety features. I'll probably make 50,000 in the next six months from that job, alone. That doesn't include the royalties I get from the two computer programs I've sold in the last couple of years."

"Dollars?" Mibs' eyes widened as she pondered earning that much income in half a year for one job.

"Don't act so surprised. The antique shop is just a hobby to me." He shrugged. "But I do have to make enough at the place to pay my cousins their salaries and cover the utilities.

How about you reimburse me for the amount I paid? $250."

Mibs glanced at her aunt. They both knew they were getting a super bargain for a quilting machine of this quality. Turning toward her office, she said, "I'll write the check; be right back."

Chapter 23

When Mibs left the room, Tony turned to Jace. "So, you're a sergeant on the Havendale Police Force. Okay, Sergeant, explain this situation with Mibs under a security watch. Bernie told me that she witnessed a murder."

"As far as we've been able to ascertain, she's the only one who saw the killer's face. I don't want to take a chance that he may try to silence her." Jace hoped he sounded as determined as he felt.

"What can I do? My hours of work can be flexible. Let me help protect Mirabelle."

Jace heard the concern in Tony's voice. The personable Italian-American obviously cared about Mibs, who had just reentered the room. "I'll let you know."

"Here you go." Mibs handed Tony the check. "Thank you."

"Yes, Anthony. Thank you," Aunt Bernie said. "Now, would you gentlemen like to stay for dinner?"

"I planned on asking you ladies if you'd go out to dinner with me," Tony announced. "I want to celebrate the software contract I signed today."

"Oh, well..." Mibs cast a glance at Jace.

"It's better if the ladies stay out of public areas as much as possible for a few days," Jace cautioned. "Give the department a chance to catch the shooter." Jace's expression softened.

"I don't want anything to happen to them."

Tony nodded. "Right. No problem. We'll order in." He added with a smirk, "I guess you can stay too, Trueblood."

Jace quipped back, "How hospitable of you, Vitali!"

Squeezing Mibs' shoulder, Jace said, "I'll go tell Officer Clarkson he can take off the next few hours. I'll stay until the next security officer shows up at nine o'clock."

When he returned from dismissing the officer on duty, they ordered Mexican carry-out.

Mibs passed out soft drinks, and Bernie pulled out Scrabble, suggesting that they challenge each other's linguistic ability after dinner.

They opened the dictionary a few times to check the correct spelling. All the players seemed to have an extensive vocabulary. However, after two hours of good-natured competition, Aunt Bernie and Jace slipped steadily ahead of the other two. Bernie was ahead by eleven points until Jace used the last of his letters, putting down the word *maximize*, normally worth 28 points, but with the double word square, it was worth a whopping 56.

Mibs' cell phone hummed with a text message from her friend, Whitney. "Wow, unbelievable!" She gasped.

"What is it, dear?" her aunt asked.

"It's a photo from Whitney." Mibs turned

the phone so her aunt could see the picture. Whitney had forwarded a snapshot of a young woman at the same formal dinner she and her parents were attending.

"Amazing," Bernie said, passing the phone so Jace and Tony could see, too.

After studying the photo, Jace asked, "Was this taken while you were in Metrofield visiting Whitney during the Fourth of July holiday?"

Mibs shook her head. "She took it just a few minutes ago. It isn't me! Whitney is at a charity function with her parents at some elegant reception hall tonight, right now."

"Let me see that picture." Tony held his hand out, taking a moment to scrutinize the photo. "It's not you, but she could pass as your double."

Bernie cleared her throat. "Whitney had mentioned before that she'd seen a girl who resembled you. Did Whitney say if she learned the young lady's name?"

After chewing on her lower lip for a moment, Mibs shook her head. "No. Maybe I'll call her tomorrow." Taking the cell phone back and setting it face down on the table, her eyes lingered on Jace. "I don't want to dwell on it now." The idea of a lookalike obviously upset Mibs. "Actually, I'm tired. I know it's still early, but I didn't sleep well last night. Would you mind if I call it a day?"

"Whatever you want, sweetheart." Jace stood. "I'll walk you over to the stairs."

"Goodnight, Aunt Bernie." Mibs gave her a quick hug. "Goodnight, Tony. Thanks for bringing the sewing machine over." Then Mibs leaned over and rubbed behind Shadow's ears.

"Get some sleep, Wonderful."

When they reached the steps, Mibs smiled at Jace. "I love you."

He ran his hand through her soft hair and kissed her. "I love you." As she moved up the steps, he smiled.

When Jace returned to the table, he found Bernie standing, leaning on her cane. "I'm heading to my room, too. You, boys, finish your drinks; stay as long as you like." She turned to Jace. "Will you make sure everything is locked up when you leave?"

"I'll do that, Bernie. Sleep well."

"Goodnight, Tony."

"I'll see you sometime soon, Aunt Bernie," he responded.

Jace sat down and finished his ginger ale, drumming the fingers of one hand in a slow rhythm. "Tony, I thought about your offer of help."

"Yeah? Do you have something in mind?"

"They don't have an alarm system set up here. Mibs said it's in Monahan's budget plans for next year. I don't want them to be without one that long. Mibs can get miffed at me later for spending the money, but I want to get it installed now, something that covers not only the doors but the windows, too." Jace recalled how a stalker had broken into the back window last year, gaining entrance and sneaking up to Mibs' small upstairs apartment. Fortunately, with the help of her indomitable aunt armed with her sturdy cane, the young woman fought off the attacker. "You're good at computers; how about electrical wiring?"

"That would be a yes," the man declared. "How state-of-the-art do you want to go?"

"Good enough that the ladies get a quick, loud notice if anyone tries to break in." Sitting forward, he added, "And one that has a silent alarm sent out, too."

"Okay." Tony grabbed the pad and pencil they had been using for the Scrabble game. "Unless you have a model in mind, I'll do some research and check reviews. I'll have some details for you in..." He stopped to glance over at Jace. "How soon do you want it?"

"The sooner, the better."

"All right, I'll have the information by the end of the day tomorrow." Tony paused. "You want me to cover the cost of this system?"

"No, this is something I should've done already." Jace focused on the man he'd met only a few hours ago, and whom he now genuinely liked. "However, I would appreciate assistance in getting it installed." Jace ran his hand through his hair. "There's one other thing." He hesitated, weighing whether he should broach another subject with this guy who claimed to consider Mibs an almost sister.

Tony leaned forward. "Does the other 'thing'

have to do with the picture that Mibs' friend, Whitney, sent here tonight?"

Jace nodded. "I'd like to get a copy of that photo and see if I can find out anything about this lookalike girl. I'm wondering if something may show up on facial recognition."

Tony cleared his throat. "I already have the picture."

"What? You do?"

"Yeah, I emailed it to myself when I held her phone a few minutes ago. What's your phone number? I'll forward it to you."

After getting Jace's number and hitting send, Tony said, "Okay, Mr. Detective, you find out what you can, and I'll use my software. You'd be surprised at what we can find online."

"Listen, Vitali," Jace cautioned, "if we find anything, we make sure it's not something that will hurt Mibs. If there's even the slightest chance that anything or anyone we might find would make her unhappy, we keep it to ourselves. Agreed?"

"Agreed." Tony held out his hand. "We'll work together, share what, if anything, we find."

Jake checked his watch. "The officer on night security should be here in about twenty minutes. "How about you grab that pad and pencil and make notes on the number of windows and doors we need to cover with the alarm system? While you do that, I'll make sure everything is locked up."

Tony grabbed the paper, and Jace gathered the empty cups to put in the sink.

"Come on, Shadow," Jace called. Shadow stretched her long, muscular frame and joined her human companions. The trio patrolled the small shop and gathered the needed information. Ten minutes later, the two men exited and locked the back entrance.

As Jace accompanied Tony to his car, he scanned the back lot and rear of the building. He planned to check the rest of the way around the building on his way to his truck. Then, he'd wait for the expected patrol car.

"You know, Vitali, I'm going to research your background tomorrow when I'm at the station," Jace said.

"Hmm. That doesn't surprise me," Tony said. "You know I'll do a search on you, too."

Before Tony shut the car door, Jace asked, "By the way, why do you call Mibs 'Wonderful'?"

Tony gave a wry smile. "Now, you wouldn't want me to reveal all of Mibs' and my childhood secrets, would you?"

Chapter 24

The following day, Jace was at his desk when a brisk knock on the open office door interrupted his concentration.

"Sergeant Trueblood," Detective Delgado addressed him with enthusiasm. "We got a ballistics match on the bullet from the theater shooting."

"What did they find, Gene?" Jace waved the detective in.

Placing the report in front of the senior officer, Delgado explained, "The slug we found at the scene matches one from a murder victim in a town up north called Juleen. That shooting is still an open case; the police department there is still hunting for the killer."

"Juleen? Why does that sound familiar?" Jace pulled out his small soft-sided notebook and paged through it, stopping near the end. "Juleen, that's the city where Michael Roberts' ex-wife now lives."

"The guy who got wounded in the shoulder?"

"Yep." Jace grabbed his suit jacket from the back of his chair. "Where is Mendoza?"

"He's out double-checking the alibi for one of the suspects who wrote threatening letters to the lawyer, Beam."

"In that case, you're coming with me," Jace directed Delgado. "I think Roberts is still home letting his shoulder heal."

"Yes, sir," Delgado responded.

Jace stopped to tell the desk sergeant where they were going. "Brice, do a background check on Roberts, Shelia–and anyone associated with her. Here's her last known address." Jace grabbed a piece of paper and copied the information from his notes, sliding it toward the sergeant.

It was a ten-minute drive to the apartment complex where Mike Roberts lived on the far edge of town. Jace parked his truck beside the building, and the two men walked to the door with the number of Roberts' apartment stenciled in black across the front. Delgado rang the doorbell.

When Roberts opened the door, a puzzled tone highlighted his words. "Detectives, what can I do for you?"

"May we come in, Mr. Roberts?" Jace asked politely.

"Sure." Stepping back, Mike gestured inside.

Jace quickly scanned the room and saw simple furnishings, neat and clean but with a lived-in feeling. Other visible areas included a kitchen and a hallway, likely leading to bedrooms and a bath. Turning to Michael, Jace asked, "How's the shoulder doing? Healing okay?"

"Pretty well. The doctor wants me to give it a couple more weeks. Then I'll start physical therapy." Roberts moved over to an oversized stuffed chair and eased into it, slowly lowering himself. Although he appeared to be downplaying the gunshot wound, the man winced, obviously still in pain. "Sit down, if you like," he offered.

"Is your son here?"

"No. Mason is visiting a friend," Roberts said, "but I doubt that you came here to ask that. What's going on, Detective Trueblood?"

"This is Detective Delgado."

Roberts nodded to him.

Michael waited for Jace, who explained, "We matched a slug we found at the theater to a shooting that happened last month in a city about four hours from here, the city of Juleen."

"What?" The man leaned forward, his eyes wide. "That's where my ex-wife lives; at least that's where she last was." Roberts peered from one detective to the other. "Are you saying Shelia had something to do with the shooting?" He shook his head. "I know she can be vindictive, but this is hard to believe. I don't think she wants Mason back. If she did, she'd take me to court. It doesn't make sense." The man covered his mouth. "Oh, man! If I was the actual target, that means that Jacob Beam was the one who got shot by accident!"

"We don't know that yet," Jace stated. "He could still have been the target. We aren't dismissing that idea, but the connection with your ex-wife's address is an interesting coincidence."

Detective Delgado cleared his throat. "Is there any reason other than your son that she'd come after you? Or is there anyone connected to her that would have a grudge against you?"

Roberts shook his head, then stopped. "Wait a minute." He got up slowly and headed to a small desk in the corner of the room. He pulled open the middle drawer and rummaged through the contents. He removed an envelope, turned, and held it out to Delgado, who had followed him across the room. "The guy Shelia is living with, James Milton, wasn't happy when my buddy took these pictures. Milton was high on drugs at the time, and he commented about his father not wanting bad publicity." Holding up his hands in bewilderment, Roberts said, "I threatened to use them if Shelia fought me for custody of Mason. She never showed up for the hearing, so I didn't show the pictures to anyone. I forgot about them until now."

"What do you think?" Delgado passed the photos to Jace.

Roberts rubbed his chin. "Don't know if there is any connection, but we had an attempted break-in yesterday. I'd just pulled into the driveway and noticed a guy messing with the side door to my apartment. As soon as I jumped out of the truck and yelled, he took off. Unfortunately, I wasn't in any shape to chase after him, so he got away."

"Did you call it in?"

"I did, Detective," Roberts said. "But I agreed with the officers who showed up that it appeared to be a random burglary attempt.

There were some scratches on the door, where the person tried to break the lock. But since he never got in, it didn't seem like a big deal." Roberts paused. "Do you think someone was after those? Who would care about them? And what would be the reason for shooting me?"

Jace focused on the solidly-built man and mentally assessed him. He didn't see the middle-aged retired veteran, father, and skilled worker as anything other than what he appeared to be–a decent, hard-working person. But the detective knew that even decent people sometimes upset others and attracted enemies. "I'd like to keep these pictures, Mr. Roberts. Nothing may come of them, but we'll start investigating and let you know if we find anything of importance."

"Sure," Roberts replied.

"Until I know for certain whether or not you were the intended victim, I think we need to put you under protective custody."

Wrinkles deepened on Roberts' face as he squinted at the detective. "Do I need to worry about somebody coming after me? What about my son?"

"Until we find out, you've got a choice. Do you want to go to a safe house or have a security detail hang out here with you?"

Mike sighed. "Let me pick my son up and see what he wants to do."

"I'm going to have Detective Delgado stay with you until I see who else is available."

Jace eyed Gene Delgado, who nodded.

"When you and Mason decide what works best for you, we'll take it from there."

As soon as Jace left the house, he phoned Sergeant Long. He waited for the desk sergeant to answer and climbed into his truck. He slipped the key into the ignition but didn't start the engine.

"Sergeant Long, Havendale Detective Division. How can I help you?"

"Brice, it's Jace. Did you get that information on Shelia Roberts?"

"Yep," the desk sergeant responded. "Shelia Roberts resides with a man named James Milton. She's currently working at a dress boutique. I didn't find any wants or warrants on her."

"What about Milton? Anything show up for him? And how about Milton's father?"

"There wasn't a lot on James Milton. There was more on the parent, James Milton, Jr; the son is Milton III. The information states that the younger Milton barely graduated from college with a degree in economics. He does have a juvenile record, but it appears those charges were dropped. He worked for his dad's company for a short time, and I can't tell if he quit or was let go. Since then, it seems he's been living on his substantial allowance. However, his father is an overachiever, CEO of a technology company, sits on the city council and on several charity boards. There are ads on the local television with him running for head of the city council. Found several articles that imply that he has higher political ambitions for his future."

"So, I'm betting his father wouldn't want any negative publicity coming up, even from his less than ambitious son," Trueblood said. "I'll be back at the station with y'all in a few minutes. But, first, I'm going to make a call."

After having a long conversation with a member of the Juleen Detective Division, Jace decided to make the four-hour trip up north. First, he went to the Havendale Police Station. Jace walked down the hall to Lieutenant Hank Taylor's office, knocked, and waited for a response.

"Enter," the lieutenant called out. "Jace, come in. What's up? Any news on the shooting suspect?"

Jace pulled back an empty chair in front of the desk and sat down. "We may have a lead, but I need to confirm if the information is reliable." He explained that the town of Juleen offered a connection between the slug from the theater and the town where Roberts' former wife, Shelia, lived. "I talked with the police captain there, and I'd like to go up and do some investigating."

Taylor nodded. "Okay. Are you taking one of the men with you?"

"Mendoza seems to have gotten used to my way of working. He's usually my first choice."

Opening his desk's left-hand drawer, Taylor

pulled out a charge card and handed it across the desk. "Take this. Keep it for future department expenses."

"All right." Jace slipped the card into his pocket, then crossed his arms. "Hank, I hope we find the guy who shot Roberts and Beam soon. Until he's apprehended, Mibs Monahan and quite possibly Michael Roberts could both be targeted."

"Are we putting a guard with Roberts?" Lieutenant Taylor asked.

"Delgado called in a few minutes ago. Apparently, Michael Roberts and his son are leaving town temporarily. They're going to stay with a couple of friends. I have his planned location, but it will be off the record. His two buddies are both active duty military, so Roberts feels they will be safe with them, especially if no one knows where they're going."

"Good," Taylor said. "And we have security at Monahan's?"

"Yep." Jace stood up.

"Hold on a minute, Jace," the lieutenant said. "I have something else I want to tell you. I'd planned on talking to you before I left work today, but since you're leaving, I'll mention it now."

"What's up?"

Hank Taylor sat back and placed his hands flat on the desk. "The captain is retiring, and I'm getting promoted to replace him."

"Hey! Congratulations, Hank. You'll make a great captain."

"Thank you," Taylor said. "The other news is that beginning the first of next month, you'll also have a new rank."

Jace's eyes widened. "I will?"

"The captain plans on making the announcement next week. You'll keep the position of Chief of Detectives, but with a new title." He stood up and extended his hand. "Congratulations, Lieutenant."

Jace slowly accepted the outstretched hand. "Sir, I haven't been here that long."

"Nevertheless, you've more than proven yourself," Taylor emphasized. "Unless we brought someone in from outside the unit, the only other two members of the detective division who might even be considered are Long and Mendoza. Mendoza has four years of experience as a patrolman and two as a detective. You have almost twice that much time in law enforcement. Sergeant Long doesn't want the position. He likes being able to go home to his kids most nights."

Jace cleared his throat and raised an eyebrow. "So, you think the team will be okay with me moving up to lieutenant?"

"I already talked to Long and Mendoza. They both think it's a good fit, and they're ready to back you up. They're keeping the news quiet for now. The rest of the group seem to be happy with your directions, so I don't see any problems." Taylor paused. "It'll mean more paperwork and less time on the street. Although you'll still go to crime scenes when needed, especially major crimes."

Opening a folder, he turned it so Jace could see the file, which included a picture of a woman; dark hair, chestnut-toned skin, brown eyes. Her name was recorded as Evening Star (Eve) Clearwater. "I want to add a new detective to our team. She's a seasoned police officer. Her husband's business transferred him to Havendale two months ago, and she's been driving back and forth to her current job, two hours each way. Detective Clearwater has applied to our department and several other police departments closer to Havendale. With her solid record, first as an officer on the street and then as a detective, I think she'll be a good addition to our team."

Jace scanned the folder and nodded. "We should bring her on before some other town grabs her."

"Hold all this under your hat until the announcement," Taylor directed. "Now, go ahead and get out of here and follow those leads you have."

Before heading out of the station, Jace returned to his desk and dialed Mibs' cell phone number.

"Hello, Jace," Mibs said after the first ring.

"Hi, Mibs." Jace smiled when he heard her voice. He decided to save the news about his promotion until he could tell her in person. "I wanted to let you know that I have to head out of town. It'll be late when I get back, or I may stay overnight, depending on what I find. I'll leave Shadow with you and Bernie tonight if you don't mind."

"We don't mind at all. I noticed that Aunt Bernie moves the dog's bed into her room when Shadow stays overnight. I think my aunt likes the company."

Jace chuckled. "That doesn't surprise me. Bernie will quickly have that dog spoiled."

"Honey." Mibs was silent over the phone, and Jace wondered why.

She cleared her throat. "I wanted to tell you that I'm heading over to the community theater tomorrow. Mrs. Barns phoned everyone working on the play. She talked to the young actors and their parents, and all but a few of them wanted to keep rehearsing for the play. I need to go over and work on the rest of the costumes." Mibs became quiet.

After glowering a bit, Jace acknowledged her comment. "Okay, but I'd prefer you don't drive yourself over. Hold on a minute." Tapping on the keys of his computer, he pulled up the next day's work schedule. "Jameson and Harte are on security tomorrow. I'll talk to them, and you make sure you don't take any chances."

"You be careful, too." He heard Mibs sigh on the other end of the phone. "Hopefully, I'll see you tomorrow."

"I'll try to call tonight if I can."

"Okay," Mibs said. "I love you."

Juan Mendoza entered the office just as Jace began to respond.

Turning his head away from the other detective, Jace whispered, "I love you, too."

Ending the call, he turned around, finding Juan smiling at him. "What?"

"Nothing." Juan cleared his throat before adding, "How is Miss Monahan today?"

Jace couldn't get upset with Juan's lighthearted words. Not long ago, Jace had been the one doing the teasing when Juan had shown interest in Mibs' friend, Whitney.

"Mibs is fine." Jace eyed his fellow detective. "Juan, I'd like you to go out of town with me to check out some information connected with the slug we recovered. We're expected at the Juleen Police Station this afternoon. I'm not sure if we will get back tonight or tomorrow. You okay with that?"

"No problem," Mendoza responded. "I keep my 'go' bag in the car."

By late afternoon, they reached the Juleen Police Department. Jace and Juan spent less than an hour at the Juleen station before they accompanied Sergeant Wilcox to the apartment leased by James Milton III.

Their knock was answered by an attractive woman, early thirties, with dark hair and blue eyes.

Chapter 25

"Shelia Roberts?" Jace asked.

The woman ran her eyes over the three men and hesitantly nodded. "Yes. Who are you?"

Even though the badge clipped to his belt was visible, Jace held it up. "I'm Detective Jace Trueblood, and this is Detective Mendoza." Indicating the third law officer accompanying them, Jace identified him as Sergeant Wilcox from the local police department. "We'd like to talk to you, please."

She blocked the door and glared. "What about?"

"About the shooting of your former husband, Michael Roberts," Jace told her.

"What?" The sneer disappeared, and her mouth fell open. "Is he hurt badly? What about Mason? Is my son okay?"

"May we come in, Ms. Roberts?"

The woman opened the door wider and moved out of the way. "Come in."

When they stepped into the house, Shelia collapsed into a chair. "Please, tell me how Mason and Mike are doing."

"Mason is fine. He was there but was not hurt. His father was wounded. After surgery and a stay in the hospital, he's home recuperating," Jace said.

Shelia blinked. "What happened?"

"That's what we're investigating," Jace responded. "We've discovered that the shooter used a gun traced to this city, to Juleen."

"Here?" Ms. Roberts' eyes widened. "You...you aren't implying that I had anything to do with it, are you?"

"We're just following leads," Mendoza explained. "Can you tell us where you were last Tuesday?"

The woman's hands trembled. "I can't believe you would think that I would hurt Mike. Just because I divorced him doesn't mean that I'd want anything bad to happen to him."

"Ma'am, please answer the question. Can you prove your whereabouts last Tuesday?"

Slowly nodding, the ex-wife squinted and pursed her lips. "Tuesday? I work on Tuesdays. I haven't missed work for over a month. I must have been there."

"May I have your work information? We'll confirm it."

As she gave Detective Mendoza the requested address and phone number, Jace studied her. "It's likely that someone hired the shooter." He watched the woman's face for any changes in her expression. "Do you know anyone who may have a reason to attempt to murder Michael Roberts?"

Shelia shrugged as tears formed in her eyes. "No. I don't." Her eyes suddenly widened. "Wait! You said someone might have hired a killer. Are you implying it could have been me?"

"We aren't making any accusations. We're

just investigating everything with an open mind," Juan replied.

"What about your current boyfriend, James Milton?" Jace asked.

"Why would James want to hurt my ex-husband?"

"You tell me," Jace countered.

Before the woman could answer, the front door opened, and who Jace suspected was James Milton III entered the apartment. He stopped and stared at the detectives.

"What's going on, Shelia?"

Jace turned. "Mr. Milton?" He once again pulled out his identification. "I'm Detective Trueblood."

"What are you doing here?" A scowl quickly spread across his features. "Get out of my home!" His face flushed red.

"Ms. Roberts allowed us in," Jace calmly stated. "We've been asking her some questions, and we'd like to talk to you, too."

"Well, I don't want to talk to you."

Wilcox stepped back to the side.

Milton added, "All of you, get out."

"Fine," Sergeant Wilcox said. "We'll move the questioning down to headquarters." He motioned to James Milton, then turning to Shelia, he added, "You too. Let's go."

Milton's eyes widened. "I'm—I'm not going."

"You can come voluntarily, or I'll take you in as a person of interest," Wilcox responded, stepping closer and getting into Milton's face.

Shelia asked, "Detective Trueblood, you said

that the gun that the shooter used was connected to Juleen. In what way?"

Jace considered her question before responding, "We found that the same gun used to shoot two men in Havendale was used in the murder of a drug dealer named Hector Jones."

"Hector Jones!" she gasped.

The three lawmen exchanged glances. Jace asked, "You recognize that name?"

"Don't say anything, Shelia!" Milton screeched.

Her face paled as she stared at her boyfriend. "What did you do, James?" she asked in a barely audible voice.

"I said shut up!" he demanded.

"Ms. Roberts, do you have something that you need to tell us?" Jace asked.

With Milton glaring at her, Shelia cowered, her head down.

Twenty minutes later, at the police station, James Milton III was sequestered in one interrogation room. Shelia Roberts waited in another. Milton refused to talk, even when they showed him one of the pictures that Michael Roberts had given to the detectives.

After plopping one of those pictures down in front of Shelia, it took only a few minutes to convince her to explain her reaction to the name Hector Jones. She confessed that Jones was the drug dealer who supplied James Milton with his narcotics. Shelia insisted that her drug use had ended after seeing those photos from Mike. They had made her realize that Mason was better off with his father and that she needed to clean up her life. "That's when I got a job and started saving my money. I hope that I'll be able to live independently and make a better life for myself soon." She paused before asking, "Why would Milton want to hurt Mike? James is happier without Mason living with us. Why try to eliminate my ex-husband?"

Jace listened as Sergeant Wilcox queried, "What about Milton's father, James Milton Jr.? I understand that he has political ambitions. Has he ever said anything about how his son's actions would affect his run for office?"

Ms. Roberts chewed on her nails, finally casting a glance at one detective, then the other. "I've only met his father twice. I've heard him tell James that he would cut off all his money if he did anything to embarrass him or cause problems with his political efforts. But I can't imagine that James would resort to...to murder just to keep his father from finding out he's a drug user."

Jace suggested, "I wouldn't say it's just the fact that his father would find out, but the fact that he would cut off all financial funds to his son."

Both men left the room and joined another detective who, along with Mendoza, had interviewed James Milton. After comparing notes and discussing that Milton still refused to talk, they decided to keep the suspect overnight. The state allowed up to 72 hours before bringing charges. There was little doubt in Jace's mind that Milton and the shooter were connected, but he had no proof that he'd hired someone to shoot Michael Roberts or Jacob Beam. Someone else could have set up a contract. Hopefully, before the allowed holding time elapsed, either the arrogant rich guy would confess, or someone would uncover proof of his involvement. Or evidence would point to someone else, possibly Samuel Hannity.

Shelia Roberts was dismissed, told not to leave town, and given a ride home. It was late when Mendoza and Jace left the Juleen Police Station. They checked into a nearby hotel that night and returned to the local police building in the morning. James Milton still refused to talk. Unless things changed, he would be released the next day.

Jace realized that there wasn't much else to be done in Juleen, so he decided they would head back to Havendale. While Jace drove, he told Juan to complete his notes. Then he called Lieutenant Taylor to relay their findings.

Chapter 26

Officers Kiel Harte and Rob Jameson had taken over guarding Mirabelle Monahan at seven o'clock that morning. They parked where they had a view of both the back and front entrance of the building. Every hour, one policeman would walk around the shop, doing a careful check of the area. The other officer would stay in the car or drive around the block, scanning the streets and rooftops.

Shortly after 10:00 a.m., Mibs stepped out of the store and waved at the patrol car. Detective Trueblood had talked to the two policemen the afternoon before, instructing them to accompany her to the theater today and reminding them that she was an eye-witness.

A few minutes later, Officer Harte helped Mibs load a container of costumes and her sewing box in the trunk. As they did that, Officer Jameson kept his eyes roving around the parking lot, watching for anyone who shouldn't be there. The person who had killed one man and wounded another was still out there somewhere.

When they reached the Havendale Community Theater, the patrol car pulled up to the front steps. Jameson accompanied Mibs into the building while Harte parked the vehicle and brought the containers inside. Officer Jameson stationed himself near the front door; he patrolled the theater floor at staggered times, ending back at the entrance. Officer Harte remained close to Miss Monahan in a spot where he could watch the back entrance and keep her in sight.

Within the next half-hour, those who needed to complete their costumes for the play had entered the theater. Each time the front door opened, Jameson scrutinized the newcomers. Fortunately, everyone seemed to belong.

~~

While others helped the younger children with their costumes, Mibs worked with her group and their outfits.

"Miss Monahan, thank you!" Wally exclaimed. "This feels better to me." The enthusiastic boy playing the part of the Cowardly Lion rushed over and hugged Mibs.

Pleased with his positive reaction, Mibs patted him on the back. "You're going to make a great Cowardly Lion. Have you been practicing your lines, Wally?"

"Yes, Mom helps me practice every day."

Mrs. Meadow nodded. "I'm very proud of how hard he's been working."

Since Mrs. Barns asked that the finished costumes stay at the theater, Mibs directed Wally and his mother to head back to the changing room to remove the outfit and hang it in the assigned area.

The next young thespian to step up for what should be a final fitting was Lena in her Good Witch costume. The pre-teen girl looked lovely in her outfit. It dawned on Mibs that she should take a picture of her as an example to show at her sewing shop. Mibs wondered whether she should start a display scrapbook. Photos of the characters from *The Unclassical Wizard of Oz*, and previous images of her work, like the picture of the wedding dress she had created, would make a great album.

Mibs turned to catch the Cowardly Lion before he reached the changing area. "Wally, wait a minute. I'd like to take your picture while you're in costume." Mibs then took a photograph of each of the outfits she—with the help of her new employees—had created.

Angie, the Scarecrow, was fetching in her overalls and plaid shirt. The straw hat topped off the girl's curly hair perfectly. Mason wasn't there to try on the Wicked Witch costume, but thinking of the last fitting, Mibs was sure the outfit would fit Mason well. The only one who needed minor adjustments was the Tin Man.

After getting individual photos, Mibs asked the young actors to pose for a group picture. Several monkeys and munchkins who were running around the stage were chased into the photo too. She planned on getting another cast picture that included Mason when he returned once the police caught the shooter.

Mrs. Barns had entered the area while they were gathered on stage and insisted they take another set of pictures. One was with her and Mr. Stewart.

Another featured Mibs surrounded by the

children wearing her beautiful creations.

After completing the picture-taking, Mrs. Barns escorted the kids and their parents to the door. The theater board had decided to treat the young actors to a pizza lunch. Mr. Stewart would be accompanying them on the outing.

When the children left, Mibs gathered her things. She left behind a small container with notions and other sewing items if she needed to make last-minute repairs.

Anita called to Mibs, "Miss Monahan, would you please send me a copy of the pictures you took? We may be able to use some of them for publicity." She paused. "I especially want a copy of the one with the whole group in it!"

"Of course. Do you want me to text the pictures or send them by email?"

"I'll give you the theater's email address. That would allow us to print them here on site. Come to the office with me, and I'll write down the address."

Officer Harte interrupted their conversation. Addressing Mrs. Barns, he said, "Ma'am, there's a delivery truck here. The driver has some type of big plants he wants to bring in. Is he expected? I'm not letting him in unless he's approved to be here."

"Oh! Yes, yes!" she told the policeman. "We are expecting a delivery of artificial bushes to use in some of the scenery." Mrs. Barns motioned to Mibs. "I'll be back in a minute to get you the email information."

Two delivery men wearing green jackets and caps pulled a low, wide cart filled with potted shrubbery onto the stage. Anita Barns scurried about, directing them where she wanted the bushes set. After they unloaded the order, one guy took the cart back for a second load while the other helped the director move several pots.

~~

Officer Harte watched the commotion for a few minutes. He checked on Miss Monahan's whereabouts. She had wandered over to the area's far edge and was studying the Emerald City set pieces. Nothing seemed amiss, so Harte stepped to the edge of the stage and gave his partner a short wave. Jameson nodded back, indicating that everything off stage was clear.

~~

Mibs heard someone call.
"Ma'am, could you give me a hand with this potted plant?" someone requested.
Mibs peered over to where she heard the voice. One of the green-coated delivery men had his back to her, turning his head slightly. He said, "I just need someone to slide the pad under this container."
"Sure, I'll help you," Mibs answered. She approached the man and bent down to reach the thin piece of cork padding. "Just lift when you're ready, and I will slide it under." Mibs' breath caught as she turned her head and stared into the eyes of the same man who had

previously pointed a gun at her.

Before Mibs could react, the vicious assailant plunged a knife into her back. Then, as she fell, he stabbed her a second time.

~~

Distracted by a loud scream, the perpetrator quickly stood up and headed for the curtained area behind the scenery. The cry had come from an older woman as she witnessed the attack. She threw a box of playbills at him, screamed again, then fainted. The package she'd thrown hit the man's arm, causing him to drop the knife. The knife bounced off a wooden stool and skidded across the floor. With no time to retrieve the weapon, he fled.

~~

Jameson reacted quickly, running forward, skipping the steps, slapping the stage floor, and pulling himself up. When he reached his partner seconds later, he saw Harte tear a piece of material loose from a display and fold it into a thick square. Pressing the cloth on the wounds, trying to stop the bleeding, he turned with a pallid face. "Ambulance! Hurry!"

As soon as the 911 dispatch answered, Jameson called for EMS, giving all the needed information. "Get me some towels, more cloth, something," he demanded of a man who had hurried over to help. Jameson placed his hands on his partner's shoulders. "Kiel, how bad is it?"

Glancing up, Kiel shook his head. "Bad." He ordered, "I got this. You go after the attacker!"

Officer Jameson hurried outside, finding one

of the delivery men leaning over a second guy. "What happened? Is there a third person with you?"

The man gaped at the policeman. "This is Joey. He and I are the only ones that came today. I thought he was out here filling the next cart. I found him like this."

Joey held his hands to the back of his head and moaned. "I got hit from behind. Saw nothing." Looking down at his chest, he noticed that he was no longer wearing his jacket. "Where's my coat and hat?"

Jameson muttered an expletive and ran toward the back of the building. No one was in view, but a small heap of green was visible at the end of the parking lot. Quickly reaching the spot, the officer recognized the jacket and hat. The attacker had apparently discarded them before climbing over the nearby fence. Jameson grabbed a section of the chain-link fence and pulled himself up and over, landing on the other side. He scanned the area, searching for footprints. The ground was hard-packed, making tracking difficult. Just as the policeman found heel marks heading to the right, he heard a car start up. Jameson pushed his way through a row of thick bushes, then broke out of the other side in time to see the back of a white car speeding down the narrow road.

He pressed the button on his portable radio. "This is Patrol Officer Rob Jameson. I was in foot pursuit of an attempted murder suspect leaving Havendale Theater. Suspect is heading east on Palmyra Road, driving an approximately ten-year-old white Honda, last three numbers on plate 597. The driver is armed and dangerous."

Jameson then asked to be transferred to Lieutenant Taylor. After Jameson gave him all available information, the lieutenant replied that he would contact the state police; if the killer had connections to the city of Juleen, he might head back that way. Taylor added that he would also make sure they had the sketch artist's picture drawn from Miss Monahan's information. Jameson closed the connection and listened to the approaching sirens. He ran his hand over his face, took a deep breath, then retraced his steps back to the theater.

When Officer Jameson reached the side of the building, he found emergency personnel checking the injured delivery man. An ambulance pulled out of the lot, sirens screeching. Detective Delgado had started up the steps, stopping when he saw the patrolman coming his way.

"Jameson, can you fill me in on what happened here? Harte went with Miss Monahan in the ambulance."

Rob headed into the building with the detective. The disheartened officer shared the information, walking Delgado through the attack and follow-up. All the while, he prayed that the young woman who had just left in the ambulance would survive.

Chapter 27

After being informed of Miss Monahan's attack, Lieutenant Hank Taylor contacted the State Highway Patrol and relayed the information. Then, he hesitated for only a moment before dialing his chief detective's phone number. Jace and Juan were on their way back from Juleen, and he wanted to tell Jace as soon as possible.

"Jace Trueblood here."

"Jace, this is Hank. How close are you?"

"We're pulling into the parking lot now. We'll be inside in a few minutes."

"Wait for me at the entrance. I'm coming out," the subdued voice of Taylor instructed. He hung up and headed down the stairs.

Pushing the exit door open, Lieutenant Taylor saw Detectives Trueblood and Mendoza across the parking lot, heading toward him.

"Lieutenant." Trueblood reached the sidewalk. "What's up? Did we get a break in the case?"

He took a quick breath, let it out, and then he placed his hand on Jace's shoulder. "Jace, Mibs has been stabbed. She's on her way to the hospital now. Come on. I'll drive." Tightening his grip, Taylor turned Trueblood around and directed him toward his vehicle.

"What happened? How badly is she hurt?" Trueblood froze and shook off Taylor's arm. "Wait! What happened?"

Taylor nudged him toward his car. "I'll tell you on the way."

Trueblood hurried at his side, his voice rising in anxiety. "Is she going to be okay?"

Taylor jerked open his car door. "We'll find out as soon as we get there."

They sped to the hospital, lights flashing and siren screaming. Hank described what had happened.

~~

As he listened, Jace felt his blood run cold, and his hands nervously opened and closed. As soon as they reached the hospital emergency entrance, Jace pushed the car door open and jumped out before the vehicle came to a complete stop. Rushing in, he grabbed the first white coat he saw and demanded to know where they had taken the stabbing victim. Before the startled intern could answer, Keil Harte called out.

"Detective Trueblood!" Officer Harte's shirt was blood-soaked.

Jace stared at the patrolman's uniform shirt, momentarily shocked by the amount of blood on the officer's shirt. He ripped his eyes away and focused on Harte. "Where is she? How bad?"

"She's in surgery now." Harte motioned to Jace. "I'll show you the way."

~~

When Lieutenant Taylor found Trueblood and Harte in the OR waiting room, he first scrutinized the police officer who had been assigned to keep Mirabelle Monahan safe.

Kiel Harte peered back. The one job he and his partner had had today was to keep that young woman from harm, and they'd failed.

As if reading the patrolman's mind, Taylor didn't reprimand him. Instead, he sent the patrolman home with directions to get cleaned up and then return to the police station to write up a report. Hank regarded Jace, who sat leaning forward with his elbows on his knees, chin resting on intertwined fingers, face red with fear and anger, and eyes staring, unfocused. Like a silent sentinel, the lieutenant waited patiently with his detective.

A good ten minutes passed before Jace sat back. He muttered, "I need to let Bernie know. I should have called her right away."

"Would you like me to take care of that?" Taylor asked.

Staring blankly, Jace nodded. "Would you have Brice or Juan go over? Bernice Monahan knows both of them. She'll probably want someone to bring her here."

"Consider it done." Hank stepped a few feet away and called the station, asking for Sergeant Long. "Brice, can you have someone cover your desk? I need you to go over and personally tell Ms. Monahan that her niece is in surgery. Bring her here if she wants to come."

"Yes, sir. Right away," the desk sergeant acknowledged.

"Jace." Taylor turned back and asked, "How

about a cup of coffee? I think they have some down the hall."

"I guess. Yeah," Jace answered dryly.

Before going for the coffee, the Havendale police lieutenant headed to the nurses' station. He found a doctor leaning on the counter and filling out a form. Taylor pulled out his official identification and directed the resident doctor to come to the waiting room and give an update on Miss Monahan's condition as soon as possible.

Hank Taylor carried two cups of coffee to the sitting area and handed one to Trueblood. "Here you go, Jace. It's hot and sweet. I know you usually drink coffee black, but I figured you could use the sugar."

"Sure," Jace mumbled. "Thanks."

A short time later, the resident came into the waiting room.

As soon as Jace saw the white-coated man step toward them, he stood up. "Do you have information on Miss Monahan?"

He nodded. "I washed up, grabbed a mask and gown, and slipped into the operating room. The surgeon informed me that they'd stopped the bleeding, but she's still in critical condition. There was an extensive loss of blood, which sent her into hypovolemic shock."

"Critical condition," Jace repeated quietly. "What are her chances?"

The doctor shook his head. "I don't know. That much blood loss is extremely traumatic." He paused. "Doctor Westfield is an excellent surgeon, and there's a great surgical team helping her. They should be able to give you a more accurate diagnosis as soon as she comes out of surgery."

Lieutenant Taylor nodded in appreciation. "Thank you." The resident nodded and left.

Jace had finished his coffee and picked up a magazine and then immediately placed it back down. He ran his hand through his hair.

~~

"Jace," a shaky voice called.

He lifted his head and shifted his eyes toward the doorway. Bernice Monahan held onto Sergeant Brice Long's arm with one hand and clutched her cane with the other.

"Bernie." Trembling, Jace walked across the room and wrapped his arms around the white-haired octogenarian. "She's still in surgery. They say she's in critical condition."

Anguish flashed in Bernice's eyes before she hugged Jace.

"Let's sit down, Jace." Slipping her arm through his, she made it to a group of chairs and dropped down on one.

"Bernice, can I get you a cup of coffee?" Sergeant Long asked, then added, "Hank, Jace, would either of you like anything?"

Jace shook his head.

Hank Taylor said, "No thanks, Brice. We already had coffee."

"Maybe you could see if there is any hot tea," Bernice replied.

Brice Long returned with a cup of tea for

Mibs' elderly aunt. He had just handed over the drink when his cell phone rang. Jace watched as Long listened intently for several minutes, broken only by short questions: where? When? Then he hung up and glanced at Taylor and Jace.

Jace stood up. "What?"

"They got him! State troopers tried to pull him over, but he gave them quite a chase, and he even ran other cars off the highway. But they were able to apprehend him at the state police roadblock," Long reported. "The suspect's name is Robert Clancy."

Despite his worry, Jace's mind clicked into police mode. "Has he told them anything?"

"They didn't say, but he had a gun on him. Hopefully, the lab will match it to the slug found at the theater." Sergeant Long's brows rose. "You know, locating that lead slug helped us find the connection with the Juleen killing."

Jace nodded and remembered. "It was Mibs who'd realized that the bullet had ended up in her basket of sewing notions. And it was that clue that gave us the connection to that other shooting."

Jace turned to Lieutenant Taylor and pulled up numbers on his cell phone, indicating a recent call. "Hank, this is the direct number for Sergeant Wilcox at the Juleen police station. Would you call him? See if he's still holding James Milton. If he is, ask him to keep Milton there as long as possible. Then we can question the suspect they just apprehended. I still believe Milton is involved in all this."

"Okay," the lieutenant said.

"Have they tracked down Hannity, the suspect who wrote the most recent threatening letters?"

"Not yet; the search is still ongoing," Taylor replied. He added, "I'm heading back to the station. Call me if either of you needs anything."

The time seemed to drag by as the small group waited for a report. They wanted someone, anyone, to come in and tell them that Mibs would be all right. Juan Mendoza replaced Brice Long. Bernice pulled out a rosary, running the green-colored beads through her fingers as she silently prayed.

Jace alternated between sitting and pacing the checkered-tiled floor. The ringing of Jace's phone broke the silence. He hesitated but finally said, "Hello. This is Jace."

"Trueblood, it's Vitali. Did you have a chance to go over the information I emailed you on security systems?"

"Tony." Jace paused, realizing that Mib's friend would want to know what had happened. "Tony...Mibs is..." Jace could hardly get the words out.

"Jace? What? What happened? Talk to me!"

"Mibs is in critical condition. She's been in surgery for over two hours already."

There was silence for half a second before

Tony declared, "I'll be there in 45 minutes." He immediately disconnected.

Another 20 minutes passed before a woman clothed in surgical garb entered the waiting area. She addressed her words to Bernice. "Ms. Monahan?"

"Yes. I'm Bernice Monahan." Bernie lifted her chin and looked up.

"I'm Doctor Joyce Westfield. We just moved your niece to ICU."

Jace offered the surgeon his empty chair. She sat down and leaned toward Bernice. "Your niece, Mirabelle, correct? Mirabelle hasn't awakened yet after the surgery. We're keeping a close eye on her, monitoring her vitals."

"Are you implying that she should be awake by now?" Bernice asked.

Sighing, the surgeon gave a slight shrug. "Normally, yes. However, with the massive blood loss, it may take longer for her body to overcome the shock. The next few days will be crucial. She's in critical condition right now."

Her voice dropping, Bernice asked, "What are her chances of waking up, of surviving?"

Jace took the seat on the other side and put his arm around Mibs' aunt.

Doctor Westfield glanced at Jace, who gave Bernie an encouraging nod. "At this point, I would say her chances are about 40 percent." She paused for a moment before continuing. "I wish I could give you a better report."

"Can we see her?" Jace asked.

Dr. Westfield stood. "I'll show you the way."

Chapter 28

Anthony Vitali peered through the glass door of Room 205 in the intensive care unit.

He saw Aunt Bernie sitting in an oversized, brown Naugahyde chair facing a hospital bed and Jace Trueblood on a metal chair on the other side. Tony studied the tall, broad-shouldered man leaning against the bed; he had slipped his hand through the bedrail and held the smaller, unmoving hand of the patient.

Tony was sure if he asked permission to join Bernie and Jace in the room, he would be told no. So he didn't ask. He quietly opened the door, stepped in, then inched closer to the bed.

His long-time friend lay still and pale, her strawberry-blond hair spread over the pillow, the sprinkling of freckles across her face standing out against the pallor of her skin. Jace glanced up and nodded in recognition.

Aunt Bernie said, "Anthony, thank you for coming."

Tony turned toward the kind-hearted, eighty-six-year-old lady, leaned down, and hugged her gently. "Aunt Bernie, how are you holding up?"

"Trying to keep hoping and praying, but my girl isn't doing too well." A tear rolled down her cheek.

"I know," he commented sadly. "I talked to a

detective in the waiting room. I think his name was Mendoza. He filled me in on everything."

Aunt Bernie nodded. "Juan is a good friend to Jace and Mibs."

Casting his gaze over to Jace, Tony said, "Detective Mendoza and another officer, I believe he said his name was Delgado, asked me to let you know someone will be waiting out there. They said the men and women from the station are taking shifts, just in case you need something." Tony held up a backpack for Jace to see, then sat it against the wall, out of the way. "Mendoza asked that I give this to you. He said it was your 'go' bag from your truck in case you wanted a change of clothes."

The detective offered a lop-sided smile. "I'll have to thank him." Sighing, Jace added, "I heard you say that Juan filled you in on what happened." With a disheartened air, he wrinkled his brow. "I should have stayed with her, Tony. I should have protected her."

"Hmph," Vitali mumbled. "I was thinking the same thing about myself." Tony studied Mibs. "I know one thing, Trueblood; Mibs is a sweet, caring person, but..." He stared at the grieving man. "She also has an independent, determined spirit. If she has something that she feels needs to be done, you aren't going to stop her."

"I've already learned that I can't keep her locked in a safe room," Jace replied. "I had a friend who told me that we can't always protect those we care about, no matter what we do."

"Sounds like a smart friend," Tony said. He ran his long, slender finger along Mibs' face. He leaned down and whispered, "Come on, Mirabelle, hang on! I know you, Wonderful. Don't stop fighting."

"Jace, while Anthony is here, why don't you take a break?" Aunt Bernie suggested. "You could even run home if you'd like."

"No!" he quickly answered. "I'm not leaving the hospital, not leaving her."

"Okay, but I think we should both get up and move around a little. Don't you?'

~~

Jace began to shake his head but stopped and considered Bernie. She had to be hurting as much as he was, perhaps more so. Mibs was everything to her; she had been her child for over twenty years. Jace thought back to the day when Bernie had told him the story of how Mibs had become not just her great-niece but also her adopted daughter.

Jace nodded. "Bernie, do you want to take a little walk? Maybe get a sandwich or something?"

"That would be good," she acknowledged.

He helped Bernie out of the chair, then offered her his arm. He gave Tony Vitali a nod and promised to be back shortly. "I should also stop and check in with my guys in the waiting area, too."

Jace adjusted his steps to accommodate

Aunt Bernie's pace. He guided her to the ICU waiting room, where he found three members of the Havendale Police Force keeping vigil.

Besides Mendoza, Jace greeted Detective Delgado and patrol officer Martha Schroeder. "Thank you, all of you, for your support. We appreciate it."

Jace addressed Schroeder, "Martha, would you take Ms. Monahan down to the cafeteria, please?"

"Bernie," he assured the older woman, "I'll be down in a few minutes. I want to catch up on activities at the station."

"Do what you need to do." Aunt Bernie patted his hand, then turned and accepted Martha's arm.

Jace broached the subject of the shooter with his associates. "Are we sure they captured the right man? Did he confess or give any useful information?"

Gene Delgado stepped forward and made a fist of triumph. "Forensics matched the gun they took from him with the bullet found at the theater and with the killing of a drug dealer, Hector Jones, in Juleen. Also, even though he wore gloves when he lost the knife at the theater, he obviously didn't have them on earlier because they found a couple of his prints on the weapon."

Juan Mendoza took over the report, saying, "Once he realized what he was up against, Bob Clancy, the suspect, started talking! He planned on making a deal with the prosecuting attorney to avoid the death penalty."

Jace's eyebrows rose. "We don't have the death penalty in this state."

"I know." Juan nodded. "But apparently, Clancy didn't realize that until later. By the time he figured it out, he'd already written and signed a confession with plenty of details."

Jace studied his partner. "Did he name Milton or Hannity?"

With an acknowledging nod, Mendoza replied, "Yes, he did. He confessed that James Milton III hired him to eliminate three people. In order to get rid of those who knew of his drug and gambling habits, he recruited him to kill Jones, Roberts, and a bookie named Albert."

"And all of this was to keep his father from finding out about the drugs and cutting off his money!" Jace bit off the words with gritted teeth. "Mibs is fighting for her life because of Milton's greed!" He breathed deeply, then reined in his temper.

"Also, they found Samuel Hannity. He'd quit his well-paying, white-collar job with one day's notice, packed up, and left town without leaving a forwarding address. Since his new job was supposed to be temporary, he hadn't bothered to fill out a change of address form, but one of our computer analysts tracked him down. Hannity had found an offshore oil company that hired inexperienced workers. He's had a temporary job for the past several months in the Gulf Coast area. When questioned by the local police, Hannity explained that he decided to leave town after his wife got a restraining order. He'd realized that he needed to move on with his life."

"So it was Roberts and not Beam that was the target," Jace stated. "Keep me up to date if you hear anything else."

"Will do, sir," Delgado promised.

"Why don't you two head back to the station? Since I'm not there, I'm sure Lieutenant Taylor could use your help," Jace suggested.

Mendoza walked to the doorway with Jace. "Jace, I wanted to mention something."

"What's that?"

"Harte and Jameson are feeling a lot of guilt for Mibs getting attacked. Neither of them has left the station since they got there. In fact, they're so keyed up, I doubt we're going to get any valuable input from them right now." Juan added, "I understand if you don't want to make any comment to them right now, but...maybe it wouldn't hurt."

Irritated, Jace closed his eyes for a second. *Why didn't they protect her better?* After a deep breath and refocusing, reality told him that there was no guarantee that any person who had been on security duty would have been able to prevent the attack. "The doctor told me that whoever put pressure on those knife wounds to stop the bleeding kept Mibs alive long enough to reach the hospital. If Officer Harte hadn't done that, she wouldn't have had any chance." Jace slipped his hands into his pockets and focused on Mendoza's face. "And tell Jameson, I'm glad he was able to get a description of the car. That enabled the state troopers to recognize and stop the vehicle."

"I think they'd appreciate knowing that."

Jace took the elevator down to the lower level and found Bernie and Officer Schroeder in the cafeteria. Although he couldn't eat much, Jace purchased a ham sandwich and a carton of milk. Forcing a few bites down, he waited for Bernie to finish her meal. He realized that she was not eating either—merely moving the food around on her plate. "Are you ready to go back upstairs, Bernie?"

"Yes, I'm ready."

"I'll clean off the table." Martha Schroeder stood and gathered the cups and plates.

"I told Juan and Gene to head back to the station," Jace informed Schroeder as he shook her hand. "Thank you."

"I'll be in the waiting area if you need anything, Sergeant Trueblood."

When she called him Sergeant, it crossed Jace's mind that he hadn't had a chance to tell Mibs about his pending promotion to lieutenant. Now, he wondered if he would ever get an opportunity.

In intensive care, they found Tony watching the monitors keeping track of Mibs' vitals. Tony glanced up as they entered. "No change."

Bernie returned to the cushioned chair.

Jace inched closer to the other side of the hospital bed, leaned down, and kissed his girl on the forehead, straightening her soft tresses before sitting down and reaching over to slip his hand over hers.

Tony paced for a few minutes before saying, "I want to buy flowers for Mibs, so she'll have something pretty to see if–when she wakes up. But I don't think they allow them in ICU."

"They may not allow flowers, Anthony," Bernie agreed. "But I remember one of my friends was able to send balloons or something to one of her relatives in intensive care."

"Maybe I can do that." He fidgeted in his chair. "I have to do something." Tony left.

~~

The faint sound of a phone tone came from Bernie's fanny pack. She had been told that wearing a fanny pack was no longer in style. She didn't care about that. The small belt purse was easier for her, considering her dependency on a cane. She zipped open the bag and pulled out her cell phone. "Hello?"

"Aunt Bernie, it's Whitney."

"Whitney!" Bernice leaned forward. "Oh, I should have called you. I guess I'm not thinking clearly. Whitney, did you hear about...?"

"I heard! Juan called me a little while ago." After dating a short while, Whitney and Detective Mendoza had kept in contact, remaining friends.

"Aunt Bernie, after my last class tonight, I'm

going to get some sleep, then I'll leave very early in the morning to start driving. I should be there before 10:00 a.m." Bernice could hear the young woman take a deep breath. "How is she doing? Is she awake yet?"

"She's still unconscious. Whitney, I don't know when I've ever been this worried!"

Silence filled the conversation as Bernice didn't know what else to add.

Finally, Whitney said, "I'll see you in the morning, Aunt Bernie. Please call if anything changes."

The evening passed by slowly. Doctors and nurses entered, checking Mibs' vitals, keeping eyes on the beeping machines. Various associates from the police station stopped by and gave encouraging words.

It was nearly 9:00 p.m. when weariness and exhaustion began to take over Bernice as she sagged against the side of the chair.

Tony, standing beside her, said, "Aunt Bernie, why don't I take you home?" Before she could protest, he said, "When Mibs wakes up, she's going to need you to be rested and ready to be strong for her."

Bernice studied the still form of her niece before responding, "Okay, Anthony. I can worry and pray just as well at home. Promise you will bring me back in the morning?"

"I'll pick you up around 9:00 a.m.," Tony said. He helped her up and then stepped toward Jace. Do you want me to come back? It might be good if you get some rest."

"Thank you, Tony, but I'm staying. Maybe I'll nap in the bigger chair for a bit. Thanks for driving Bernie home."

"No problem. Just make sure you call if there is any change," Tony said.

"I will. I have your number," Jace said. "Tony, do you need a place to sleep? You can stay at my house."

"Thanks, but no. I have a room in the back of my fix-it shop. It has a cot that I sometimes use when I'm tinkering around with stuff and it gets late."

~~

After they left, Jace scanned the room—pale-blue walls, now dark windows, the two balloons attached to the small teddy bear Tony had purchased, and the array of monitors. Sighing loudly, he rested his head on the bed rail as he held Mibs' hand and focused on the still face of the woman he loved. At some point, he fell asleep in that position. When the nurse made her rounds, entering the room to check on the patient, Jace woke up. With a stiff back and a crook in his neck, he moved over to the oversized chair to rest. Sometime during the night, someone had gently covered him with a flannel blanket.

Chapter 29

Jace jerked awake and blinked, then he focused his attention on the immobile figure lying on the hospital bed. He rubbed the sleep from his eyes, then pushed himself out of the chair. Jace gazed down at his girlfriend. He softly kissed her cheek, hoping for some kind of indication that she might regain consciousness. Her eyelids didn't open to reveal that sparkling green color. Her lips didn't move to form the sweet smile that never failed to make his heart skip a beat. The stillness pierced Jace's soul with a clenching ache. His thoughts were interrupted when a nurse entered the room. She quietly replaced an IV bag and patted Jace on the shoulder before leaving.

The clock on the wall indicated that it was just past four in the morning. Jace noticed the backpack that his fellow detective, Juan Mendoza, had thought to send over. Realizing that he'd had on the same clothes for a day and a night, he picked up the bag and headed to the nearest restroom. He changed into jeans and a polo shirt with the Havendale Police logo, then washed his face and brushed his teeth. Jace felt slightly better. His stomach growled, and he remembered that he hadn't had more than a few bites since yesterday's breakfast. He needed to find something to eat.

He entered the elevator and pushed the button for the first floor. When Jace reached the double-door entrance of the cafeteria, he saw that the area wasn't open. The only light came from the back, where indistinct noises indicated that perhaps someone was doing prep work for the morning rush. He spied a vending machine down the hall. He slipped money into the slot and bought a carton of juice and a bag of peanuts. Sitting on a bench in the lobby, he consumed his makeshift meal, promising himself he'd try to find something more substantial later. On his way back to the intensive care unit, Jace met Officer Clarkson in the hallway.

"Sergeant Trueblood, I was just leaving." The patrolman stopped. "I peeked into the ICU room a while ago, but you were sleeping in a chair, so I didn't go in. I talked to the nurse, who said there was no change."

"Mibs still hasn't woken up," Jace said.

Clarkson rubbed his chin. "Is there anything I can do? Anything you need?"

"There isn't much to do except to wait." Taking a deep breath, Jace said, "I sure do 'preciate y'all being here for me, for us." He sighed. "But I don't want y'all spendin' so much of your time sitting in the waiting room. I know everyone has better things to do."

"Hey, we'd do this for anyone on the force," the officer said. "In fact, I heard one of the crime scene techs talking about how you were at the hospital on your day off when his kid had pneumonia. You're one of us, Sergeant."

Reaching out, he shook Clarkson's hand. "Thank you."

"Kiel Harte just replaced me. He's in the waiting room," Officer Clarkson added as he headed down the hall.

Jace rubbed the back of his neck. He'd rather not talk to Harte. He wanted to return to Room 205; he needed to be back there next to his girl. He pulled himself together and wandered down the hall, turning to the left when he reached the ICU wing of the hospital. Jace stepped into the visitors' waiting area. Harte sat with his head bent toward the floor and his hands clasped. The detective watched the off-duty officer for a few minutes. He could almost feel the anguish weighing on the young man's shoulders.

"Hello, Kiel."

"Sir!" Regret and worry had the man appearing a little rough around the edges. "I'm sorry. I...ahh...no excuses."

"Kiel." Jace stopped him. "We can't undo what's done. But, hopefully, we can learn from it."

Jace motioned for the officer to sit back down and took the chair next to him. Silence filled the air for the next ten seconds before the chief of detectives spoke. "I remember an incident that happened when I was on the force in Nashville. I pulled over a car for swerving all over the road. I figured the driver was drunk. He was and couldn't even walk straight, much less pass a breathalyzer test. There were three guys in the vehicle, and it became apparent that all of them had a lot of alcohol in their systems. My partner, Jerry, and I had them all get out of the car. I checked the driver. One of the men gave Jerry a hard time, being extremely uncooperative. The third guy, a short, preppy fellow named Boulton, just stood there, so we didn't keep a close eye on him. The next thing I knew, that third guy jumped back in the car and took off."

Jace paused as he remembered that tragic day. "I threw handcuffs on the original driver and passed him off to Jerry, jumped in our unmarked car, and hit the siren. By the time I caught up with that drunk driver, he'd run a red light and plowed into a van full of young teens returning from a soccer game. I called for assistance and found Boulton passed out and trapped in his car. I hurried over to the van. All but one of the kids ended up having only minor injuries. One fourteen-year-old girl wasn't so lucky. I still remember her. Susan. She had honey-colored hair, blue eyes, wearing a brown-and-yellow-striped sweater." Jace blinked away the tears and straightened. "A piece of metal that had torn loose from the drunken man's car had flown through the open window and hit her in the neck. Cut the carotid artery. I couldn't stop the bleeding, and she bled out in my arms."

The two remained silent.

Finally, Jace faced the younger patrolman.

"For days, my mind kept seeing that young girl's blood on my hands. I kept thinking—if I had kept a better eye on that third man. If I'd done something different…if…if."

Jace stood up and scrutinized the patrolman. "Not too long ago, I was reminded that there are things you aren't going to forget, but you need to learn to file them away. If you don't, it won't be long before you are no good for anyone."

He recalled something Catherine McBride, daughter of the man who had given Jace that advice, had said. She mentioned that her father, William, had regularly attended a group session for veterans suffering from PTSD. "You know the police department recommends that when an officer goes through a traumatic event, that they take some time to talk about it. The captain has a couple people he recommends for therapy sessions."

"I'll be fine," Harte insisted. "I just feel guilty that I let this happen."

Jace considered the reluctant, nervous manner of the patrolman, quite unlike his usual professional demeanor. "Actually, Officer Harte, I'm going to make it an order. I'll ask Lieutenant Taylor to have someone contact both you and Officer Jameson."

"Sergeant, did you find someone to talk to when…after the girl in the van died?"

Reflecting on that troubled time, Jace answered, "Yes, I did. Once a week, every other week for three months, with the understanding that I'd go back if I felt the need." He added, "We're taught to be tough and self-reliant, but that doesn't mean there won't be a time when we may need to talk and listen; there's nothing wrong with asking for help."

Kiel Harte nodded. "Yes, sir. Thank you, Sergeant."

It was a little past 5:30 a.m. when Jace returned to Mibs' room. The last hour and a half were the longest Jace had been away from his sweetheart's side since she came out of surgery. He gently twirled strands of her strawberry-blond hair through his calloused hands. He whispered to her, hoping that even unconscious, she would hear his voice. Perhaps the words would spark her mind, bring her closer to consciousness.

He talked about the house he was updating, the sprawling Georgian Colonial he'd inherited from his great-uncle Ezekiel. The huge fixer-upper was a challenge to remodel. But it was a challenge that Jace enjoyed, especially on the days when Mibs joined him. He recalled the first time he'd showed her the home. They'd only had one official date at that time, but Jace had hoped that they would get a chance to spend more time together. Mibs had stayed for several hours that chilly, fall morning. She'd even helped strip the aged, peeling wallpaper from the living room walls.

The cost of a whole-house renovation would

have been more than a small-town detective's salary would cover on its own. Luckily, the inheritance included the double-lot, home and garage, *and* a substantial monetary bequest of stocks, bonds, and a high six-figure savings account. The now 33-year-old Trueblood used the money wisely. He hadn't used the inheritance for anything except restoring the property. It was only fitting that he take care of his deceased uncle's home.

The house began to resemble the stately home that it had once been. He tried to keep as much of the original design as possible. Jace had taken pains to restore what he could, including pediment, dormers, and trim. He had also sanded and recoated the original woodwork and decorative carvings around the doorways and windows. His father, Christopher Trueblood, was a retired contractor and home builder. He'd traveled from his retirement home in Arizona earlier that year to help his son restore the original marble floor that covered the large living room.

Jace's mom had accompanied Chris on that trip. That visit was the first time his parents had met Mibs. Jace had introduced other ladies to his parents in the past, but he'd realized that Mom and Dad knew him well enough to sense that there was something different about this young woman. Jace couldn't stop the way his eyes lit up when he'd spoken about Mibs or hide the enamored tone in his voice when he described her.

Jace had overheard his mom tell his dad, "I think our bachelor son finally has someone special in his life."

He had been delighted to see how his parents were immediately smitten by the energetic and friendly Mirabelle Monahan. And how Mibs had appeared at ease around his mom and dad, falling into comfortable conversation with them.

Mibs had brought Aunt Bernie with her to meet his parents. His mom and Bernie seemed to instantly click, finding dozens of things to talk about. While Chris and Jace had worked on the tile floor, the ladies sat at the kitchen island, reviewing recipes from a cookbook Anna had brought with her.

Jace remembered how happy he'd felt walking in and seeing the people he cared most about together, enjoying each other's company. He recalled how Mibs had gazed up with that sparkle in her eyes and smiled at him. Yes! *That* had been a good day.

"Mibs," Jace now said, "my dad and mom are flying in from Arizona next week. Dad's going to sort through the stuff in the garage with me. Remember? I told you that I'd taken only a quick glimpse inside that big outbuilding. I think there may be some things out there that he'd like to restore."

Because he'd wanted to concentrate on making the house livable before tackling the yard or garage, Jace had taken a quick peek into the garage when he had first moved in, then shut it back up for later perusing. Now that he had the master bedroom, kitchen, and living room done, he'd gotten curious about the massive outbuilding's contents. If there was anything of interest in there, he and his father might want to devote some time inventorying the items when they weren't working on the unfinished rooms in the main house.

He continued his soliloquy, hoping that Mibs could hear him. "I know that the dining room and the rest of the bedrooms in the house need to be finished, but I think it would be a nice break to explore that overstuffed garage. There could be some antique furniture that might be used in the house. Should I keep some of the things or get rid of them?" He felt a lump in his throat as he murmured, "I need you."

Jace stepped away to bring his emotions under control, something he was able to do quickly when working as a detective and dealing with criminals. It was easy to put on the sober, self-detached façade that detectives used when questioning a suspect. It was another thing when it came to people he cared about. Gazing out the window, he watched the sunrise pushing its way through the early-morning clouds. He slowly turned around and stepped back to the side of the bed.

"Mibs, darlin', please wake up," he begged.

He took a deep breath and slowly let it out. "Did I tell you that my Uncle Ezekiel left a

Chevy Impala parked in the garage? It was probably the last car he drove; it's like new and right inside the door, so it's easy to recognize. There's another vehicle in there too. I can't be sure until I move stuff out of the way to get to the far bay, but I think it may be a Jeep Wagoneer from the late 1980s. The tarp covering it has slipped off enough to make me think that's what it could be." Jace forced a smile. "I bet there are all kinds of interesting things in there. We could consider going through them, like a treasure hunt."

His voice droned on for quite a while, bringing up things that he thought would interest Mibs, before he finally fell silent. He walked back to the window and realized the sun had fully risen. According to his watch, it was after seven in the morning. He heard the glass door slide open, turned, and expected to see a member of the nursing staff. Instead, a tall, pretty, ebony-skinned woman in her twenties slipped through the door. The silky fabric of her white blouse and plum-colored capris made a soft, swishing sound as she walked into the room. Jace stepped over to meet the young woman and gave her a tight hug.

"Whitney! I wasn't expecting you so early."

"I woke up and couldn't go back to sleep, so I climbed in the car. Since the traffic was light, I made good time." She gazed past his shoulder and stared at Mibs, then moaned, "Oh, Jace."

Pulling Whitney closer, Jace let her lean her head on his shoulder.

"I have to keep believing Mibs is going to be okay," he said.

They talked and shared memories. After a while, Whitney insisted that Jace take a break, get a cup of coffee, take a walk, something to help him recharge. His stomach growled again, so he decided to go back to the cafeteria, which he hoped would be open by now. Exiting the intensive care unit, he ran into Lieutenant Taylor.

"Jace, how is she? Any change?"

Ill at ease with the fact that Mibs had not yet woken, Jace shook his head. "Still the same." He pointed down the hall. "I haven't eaten much the last couple of days. I thought I'd go down to the cafeteria. Care to join me for breakfast, Hank?"

"Sure," his commanding officer responded.

Chapter 30

Anthony Vitali brought Aunt Bernie to the hospital around 9:30 a.m. Tony had heard of Mibs' college roommate, Whitney, but this was the first time they had officially met. He regretted that their first meeting happened during such an unfortunate time. Nevertheless, Tony found it easy to connect with the vivacious roommate.

Tony told Jace and Whitney that things were fine at the sewing shop. He had talked to Deanna Maxwell that morning, and she felt that she could handle the store for the day. Deanna had arranged to work the whole day, staying in the afternoon to assist Mary Wong. Aunt Bernie had told the employees that if they felt the least bit overwhelmed, they had her blessing to close up and head home.

~~

A nurse entered Room 205. Since Jace had returned from his breakfast, there were now four of them in the room. The nurse was not happy about that. She reminded the group that only two people, preferably blood relatives, were allowed in the room at one time.

"Jace," Tony said. "Would you take a walk with me? I wanted to ask you something anyway."

Jace felt like he'd already been away from Mibs' side more than he'd planned that morning. But realizing that Bernie or Whitney would call if needed, Jace nodded. "Maybe we can step outside and get a little fresh air."

As the two men walked around the medical complex, Tony said, "I understand they caught the guy who did the shooting at the theater and hurt Mirabelle. Did I hear correctly?"

"Yes." Jace rehashed the information that Lieutenant Taylor had told him. "The murderer is talking in exchange for some kind of leniency."

"Leniency!" Tony exclaimed. "They aren't going to let him off, are they? Please tell me there isn't going to be some kind of witness protection or something."

"No. My understanding is that the suspect is afraid of the death penalty. The lieutenant believes that he will likely spend the rest of his life in prison without the possibility of parole."

"So? The underlying reason was money?" Tony frowned.

"Apparently, James Milton Jr. has political ambitions and gave his son an ultimatum. Milton III had to make sure that no negative publicity, nothing embarrassing, became public. If he caused the older Milton any embarrassment that hindered his plans, James Milton would no longer receive any financial support. I guess the old man had taken care of some previous less-than-stellar actions on the son's part. But instead of cleaning up his act, the younger Milton decided to eliminate witnesses to anything that he thought wouldn't pass muster with his father."

"What a self-centered, self-seeking jerk! Living the easy life was more important to him than another person's life."

Jace sighed, then started walking again. "Milton didn't pull the trigger, but he might as well have. He'll be charged with first-degree murder for hire."

Tony joined him. Even at a casual pace, the two tall men's long strides covered the walkway in front of the facility in a short time. They'd reached a small, wooded area with several benches scattered under the trees. Pausing only briefly, Jace decided to forgo the idea of sitting and continued to stroll around the shady knoll.

"So, the shooter was paid to do Milton's bidding?" Tony asked.

"The suspect's named Robert Clancy. He was a drug runner and a low-level gun for hire. Apparently, James Milton—the son, not the dad—obtained his name through his cocaine supplier, Hector Jones." As they ambled, Jace shook his head. "Milton hired Clancy to get rid of a guy named Marcus Albert, a bookie who held a 50,000 dollar note on gambling bets that Milton had made. He also had Michael Roberts on the hit list because of the fear that the photos showing Milton in a drug-induced stupor would resurface. What's ironic is that Jones, the dealer who found the gunman for James Milton, was also added to the kill list."

Tony kept mumbling something in Italian about *insensato*. Jace figured it meant something along the lines of a senseless act.

When they made the circuit back to the front of the hospital entrance, into the building, and to the elevator, Jace said, "Tony, I've got somewhere I want to go. I'll see you upstairs."

Jace made his way down the long, quiet hallway as he headed for the sign he'd noticed earlier that morning. He turned one corner, then a second, and reached his destination. Pushing open the door, he hesitated; soon, the quiet, reverent atmosphere drew him in. He walked past the wooden pews and stopped in front of the altar. For the first time in many years, Jace knelt down and gazed up at a carved, wooden crucifix.

"Lord, I know I haven't been on talkin' terms with you for a long time. Maybe blaming you when my kid brother died was my only way of dealing with the loss. But, if I'm honest with myself, I realize that pushing you away didn't bring Connor back. I was so angry. He wasn't just my brother; he was my best friend. Maybe I'm jealous because he's with you, and not with me." He closed his eyes and folded his hands. Jace took a deep breath. "I am sorry. I'm sorry for being so bullheaded, so stubborn. I'm asking you to forgive me and give me the strength to handle whatever the future brings." The sorrow for his previous self-centered attitude, combined with the fear of losing Mibs, made his chest tighten.

"Dear God, please, please don't take Mibs from me." There was a rough catch to his voice. "I know she belongs to you and has your never-ending love, but I love her too. Please let her stay with me. I want us to have a life together, to grow old together." Jace felt tears slide down his face. "Thy will be done, Lord. Just give me the grace and strength for whatever happens."

When Jace returned to the ICU, he found Tony and Whitney standing outside the waiting room, talking to Juan Mendoza.

"Jace," Juan said. "Whitney told me that she and Mr. Vitali are giving Bernie a little time to stay alone with her niece."

"We thought she needed that," Tony said. "We're also wondering if it isn't too early to talk her into going to lunch. I know that if she doesn't take a few steps every couple hours, her hip gets stiff."

Jace checked his watch. "It's after 11:00. By the time she gets down to the cafeteria and has something to eat, it will be close to noon. I think that would be a good idea."

Declaring that he would get Aunt Bernie, Tony headed back to Room 205.

Jace turned toward Juan. "Everything okay at the station, Juan?"

"Nothing major. A fender bender and a domestic complaint—nothing our division can't handle."

Jace nodded. "Juan, why don't you get lunch with the others? That would give you and Whitney a chance to visit."

"Good idea," Whitney said as she slid her hand through her friend's arm.

After leaving the small group escorting the white-haired aunt to lunch, Jace returned to Mibs' room. He moved the smaller chair beside the far side of the bed, near Mibs' arm without an IV. He sat down and gently wrapped his hand around his girl's fingers. "Mibs, if you can hear me, remember that I love you."

He tried to keep an upbeat tone and continued the one-sided conversation. After a while, he rested his head on the metal guard rail and closed his eyes.

~~

Slowly opening her eyes, Mibs waited for the bright white above her to come into focus; soon, blurry lines became the outlines of ceiling tiles. She lay quietly as her mind started to form coherent thoughts. Then she remembered the last thing she had seen before darkness set in—the face of the shooter. She gasped as she recalled the sudden pain, followed by darkness. She turned slightly left when she heard the beep of the nearby machines. She allowed her eyes to follow the lines from the monitors. They were attached to her arm. She tried to raise her other hand, but something held it down. Her lips felt dry, but she couldn't stop smiling. There weren't more medical attachments clamping her hand. Instead, strong fingers were wrapped around hers, and a tumble of curly chestnut hair partially covered the face of the person she most wanted to see. There was a stubble of beard outlining his strong jaw, something she wasn't used to seeing on her usually clean-shaven boyfriend.

Her throat was so parched that it took a couple tries before she could speak. "Jace, honey." She paused before trying again. "Jace."

~~

Was he dreaming? Jace slowly opened his eyes, thinking he heard Mibs softly calling his name. The second time her voice reached him, he knew it wasn't a dream. Lifting his head, he saw her beautiful green eyes and a weak but lovely smile on her lips.

"Jace," she whispered.

"Mibs! Sweetheart! I'm here."

He gently caressed the side of her face, then his heart raced. He wanted to say so much, but the words stuck in his throat.

The door to the room slid open, and a nurse hurried in. "I noticed on our monitor screen that her blood pressure suddenly went up and her heart rate increased." She smiled. "I'll get the doctor."

The nurse returned quickly, followed by two doctors and other nursing personnel.

To let them check Mibs' condition, Jace moved around to the edge of the room by the window. He took a deep breath as he stared out the window. The clouds were gone, and the sky was now clear and blue. Happiness filled his heart as he uttered grateful words. "Thank You, God. Thank You."

Chapter 31

In the ensuing weeks, Jace discovered that the dealer who had supplied James Milton III with his drugs was connected to the same drug cartel Jace and the task force had dismantled. Hector Jones, Milton's supplier, was one of many small-time dealers who were the final distributors of the drugs. Compared to the major players in the syndicate, the bottom of the food chain was nothing more than a small nail on the edge of a giant wheel. Either way, Jace was glad that the drug cartel was no longer in operation. Although a minor character in the drug world, Jones' death made it possible to connect Clancy to both the murder of Mr. Beam and the attempted murder of Mibs. And, of course, that led to the plea deal for life without parole.

~~

Jace reached for Mirabelle Monahan's hand as they exited the tall, open doorway of Christ the King Church. Just as he had for the last three Sundays, Jace drove Mibs and Aunt Bernie to Mass that morning. His girlfriend, steadily gaining back her strength after leaving the hospital, had insisted that she was ready for the day's activities. Bernice and Jace had combined efforts to put together a birthday party for Mibs. He knew Mibs didn't need a birthday party, but organizing and completing the project made both her aunt and him happy.

He had trouble keeping his eyes off the pretty, composed young woman by his side, so glad that she was here with him. The fear and pain of almost losing Mibs had been replaced by the simple joy of her company.

Mibs gazed up at Jace and leaned her head against his shoulder as they exited the stately Renaissance-style church.

Mibs had told him how glad she was that the children's play, *The Unclassical Wizard of Oz,* had opened as scheduled. So, he'd taken her and Aunt Bernie to yesterday's matinee. The three of them had stayed to talk after the curtain closed, and Mibs had been greeted with hugs of appreciation from several young thespians who had loved the costumes she'd made for them. Jace had stopped Mike and Mason Roberts before leaving the theater to ask them to come to Mibs' party. Jace had sensed that being attacked by the same criminal had forged a sad but close bond between Mibs and Mike. Hopefully, having a reason to celebrate would lessen the bad memories for both of them.

Jace was confident that everything would be ready when they arrived. Whitney and Juan were already at Alonzo's Ristorante, putting up decorations in the private room rented for the occasion. Bernie's friends, Hazel and Marge, had insisted on taking care of the birthday cake, three layers, each a different flavor.

He was so happy and relieved to have his girl with him that he had been tempted to invite the whole town. However, reality, along with Aunt Bernie's sage oversight, had him settle for family and friends. This included the members of the detective division that Chief of Detectives, Lieutenant Trueblood, headed and Monahan's two new employees, Deanna and Mary.

Jace's parents had changed their plans too. Instead of staying for a week, they were settling into their son's house for the next month. Jace was glad that installation of the new whole-house air-conditioning had recently been completed, making their stay more comfortable.

The father and son were having a good time exploring the oversized garage, chock full of cars, tools, furniture, and other uncovered items. Jace was glad his mom had joined with Aunt Bernie to give Mibs a lot of tender loving care as she recuperated.

Jace had talked to Bernie and knew that she was glad they'd hired the two employees. Mary and Deanna were doing a fine job of keeping Monahan's running while Mibs was off work. Especially since Bernie had insisted that, for now, they only sell materials and sewing items and take in mending, but no special sewing orders.

Jace glanced back to locate Bernie and saw

Anthony Vitali had already offered her his arm. Tony, accompanied by a friendly blue-eyed blonde, had slipped into the end of the pew just before Mass began. Jace watched Tony slow-stepping down the stairs to make it easy for Bernie as he guided the aged aunt to the sidewalk. Rachel, Tony's friend, smiled and waved when she saw Mibs and Jace waiting.

~~

"So, where did you and Rachel meet?" Mibs asked Tony as they gathered at the bottom of the steps.

"At an auction a few weeks ago," he explained. "Rachel's dad happened to be the auctioneer that day." Tony added, "Actually, Rachel is an auctioneer too. Pretty good, if I do say so."

"Well, thank you, kind sir." The girl smiled.

"Are you ready for your party, Mibs?" Tony asked. "It's not every day you turn 24."

"I'm ready." Mibs grinned at Tony. "I better be. Aunt Bernie and Jace aren't giving me a choice."

Rachel's smile filled her full, rosy-cheeked face as she reached for Mibs' arm. "Happy Birthday! Tony has talked about you enough that I feel I almost know you." The young woman's solid build and defined muscles evidenced the physical activity that filled her days. Rachel mentioned that besides helping her father set up for auctions and run other aspects of his auctioneering service, she managed a small shop called Knick-Knacks and More. She told Mibs about the consignment shop where she'd purchased the coral sundress she was wearing.

~~

Jace turned away from the girls when Tony tapped him on the shoulder, directing him to step a few feet away. "I've been doing computer research on the 'lookalike' girl in the picture Whitney sent," Tony said, "and I have some information."

Jace and Tony had put a temporary hold on finding out about the girl who lived in Metrofield and eerily resembled Mibs. However, now that Mibs was on the road to recovery, Tony had begun investigating.

"Does the information appear promising?" Jace's curiosity was piqued by the news.

"I found a name. I also found some articles about a kidnapping that happened over twenty years ago."

Jace listened to the information. When Tony stopped talking, Jace asked, "A kidnapping? What are you saying, Vitali?"

"The kidnapping involved three-month-old twin girls. They recovered one girl, but the other was never seen again, never found."

Standing still, unmoving for several beats, Jace processed the information. "Are you implying that one of those twins is the girl in Whitney's photo?"

"I'm not implying. I am stating that the girl in the picture is Camila Richmond, the baby that the FBI found and returned to her parents twenty-four years ago. The other sister, Clara, disappeared. From the reports I uncovered, two men were at the drop site where the exchange of money for the baby girls was to take place. Something went wrong; one kidnapper was killed, and only one child was recovered. A second man escaped. He was last seen entering an alley frequented by homeless people. They never located him or the second twin."

"This happened in Metrofield, the city where Marian Carpenter lived on the street for over a year?"

"The same city," Tony acknowledged. "I found a lot of details about Camila Richmond."

Scowling at the computer genius standing in front of him, Jace cautioned, "I hope you're not searchin' in places that aren't open to the general public."

Tony raised his eyebrows and tried to present an innocent expression. "Most of what I've uncovered can be found, if you know where to search." Ignoring Jace's frown, he said, "Listen for a minute. Camila Richmond has type B+ blood. I've seen Mibs' Red Cross blood donation card, so I know that's her type too. The girl in Metrofield and Mibs are the same height and have the same color eyes; they're almost identical. The reason I say almost is that there are some interesting differences."

Still frowning without commenting, Jace

waited for Tony to continue.

"Have you ever heard of mirror twins?"

"What?" Jace questioned.

"Mibs is right-handed. Camila Richmond is left-handed. Mibs has a cute little upturn to the right side of her mouth when she smiles. I can tell from the pictures I've seen of Camila she has the same feature, except on the left side of her mouth. Mibs is very artistic, while the other girl seems to be very good at math and science. She's working on a master's in engineering. Don't you see? They're like mirror images!"

Jace ran his hand through his curly, chestnut hair, considering the possibility Tony brought up. "But we know who Mibs' mother was and that she died in a car accident."

"Are we sure?" Tony queried.

Stunned by the unexpected question, Jace had not yet replied when they heard Bernie's voice.

"Tony, have you met Jace's parents?" Bernie called, interrupting the conversation as she pointed toward Mr. and Mrs. Trueblood. The couple had just finished talking to Father Smith and headed their way.

"Be right there, Aunt Bernie," Tony responded, turning back to Jace.

"We'll talk about what you discovered later," Jace said as Tony stepped away.

Tony moved up for the introductions, grabbing Rachel's arm and pulling her along with him.

Jace stepped over and put his arm around Mibs' shoulder, walking with her to where his parents stood. As Jace let his eyes wander over the assembled group, he smiled.

Mibs patted his arm, and he gave her a smile filled with both desire and uncertainty. "What?" she asked. "You appear to have something on your mind."

Jace did have something on his mind, something besides the subject that Tony had been discussing. He didn't care about Mibs' past as much as her future. Jace had been thinking about the best way, the best place to ask her something. He'd thought of different romantic scenarios, considered a candlelight dinner, flowers, and candy, even thought about donning a tuxedo. He couldn't decide on the perfect setting. But, right now, with the people who were here—his parents, Aunt Bernie, some of Mibs' friends, Father Smith, who had spent several hours lately listening to Jace and giving him spiritual advice—and this place, in front of God's house. It suddenly felt right.

"Walk with me, Mibs." Jace guided her away from the group. Stopping in front of a flower garden to the right of the stairs, he took a huge breath and let it out. Jace gazed into the sparkling green eyes of the beautiful girl he loved. "I want to ask you something." He gestured toward the friends and family standing in front of the church. "...In front of God and everyone."

Mibs' eyes widened, and her mouth opened as she watched him pull a small velvet box out of his pocket and get down on one knee.

Jace opened the ring box and held it forward. "Mirabelle Louise Monahan, will you do me the honor of being my wife?"

Mibs nodded. "Yes, Jace Ezekiel Trueblood, yes."

Jace stood and placed the single solitaire ring on Mibs' finger.

The proposal had not gone unnoticed. Cheers and clapping erupted from the group assembled in front of the church. Jace saw his father give a nod of approval. Tony and Rachel were clapping. Aunt Bernie and Jace's mom were hugging each other, both seemingly ready to cry. Other parishioners who had lingered smiled at the loving scene. And Father Smith had a big grin on his face, arms crossed, rocking back and forth on his heels.

The young couple gazed at each other, love radiating between them. Jace placed a hand on each side of Mibs' face and claimed her lips with a soft kiss.

Happiness filled his heart. "Sweetheart, I love you!"

With misty eyes, Mibs smiled. "I'll love you forever."

About the Author

Joan L. Kelly currently lives in Virginia and enjoys spending time with her daughters, sons-in-law, and especially her grandkids.

Notions of Murder is the second in the *Mibs Monahan* Cozy Mystery Series. *A Thread of Evidence* is the first.

Joan's philosophy is that life can often be difficult; fiction stories are excellent therapy. When life gets hard, escape for a while in a good book.

Previously published books, *My Big Feet, Hiding the Stranger,* and *The DNA Connection,* were written for younger readers.

Joan Kelly's YA work has been called "highly recommended for community library fiction collections" by *Midwest Book Review.*

Published by
Full Quiver Publishing
PO Box 244
Pakenham ON
K0A2X0
www.fullquiverpublishing.com